A
*Ecstasy Romance*®

# "DON'T BE AFRAID OF ME."

He leaned forward to kiss her tenderly on both cheeks, then pushed aside her hair to tease her earlobe with the exploring tip of his tongue. Raw yearning made her body quiver, and he pulled her onto his lap, sighing with contentment when she finally relaxed against him, her fingers slipping into the thick hair at the back of his head. Groaning deeply, he locked his mouth on hers, kissing her with fervor.

"I know you like this," he whispered into her hair. "Don't go cold on me again."

With ringing ears and clouded senses, she pulled his head against hers, pouring all the force of her frustration into their raging, enveloping kiss.

# CANDLELIGHT ECSTASY ROMANCES ®

# THIS BITTERSWEET LOVE

*Barbara Andrews*

*A CANDLELIGHT ECSTASY ROMANCE* ®

To Pamela, the bride

To Our Readers:

We have been delighted with your enthusiastic response to Candlelight Ecstasy Romances®, and we thank you for the interest you have shown in this exciting series.

In the upcoming months we will continue to present the distinctive, sensuous love stories you have come to expect only from Ecstasy. We look forward to bringing you many more books from your favorite authors and also the very finest work from new authors of contemporary romantic fiction.

As always, we are striving to present the unique absorbing love stories that you enjoy most—books that are more than ordinary romance.

Your suggestions and comments are always welcome. Please write to us at the address below.

Sincerely,

The Editors
Candlelight Romances
1 Dag Hammarskjold Plaza
New York, New York 10017

# CHAPTER ONE

Sara shivered, but it was excitement, not the drafty chill of the primitive barn that affected her. The team of Yankee-bred auctioneers had finally finished selling a seemingly endless assortment of farm equipment and tools, and the household items from the estate were being carried to the makeshift platform. The crowd was far larger than she'd expected on a cold November Saturday, but most of them seemed to be onlookers or practical bargain hunters, locals who scoffed at summer people and antiques dealers from big cities who paid what the natives considered outrageously high prices for bits and pieces of Vermont's history. Some spectators were making a social event of the auction, and others saw it as a sort of second funeral for Samuel Hargrove, the deceased farmer whose possessions were on the block.

For the hundredth time she cast loving eyes on the coveted prize, a turned-wood spinning wheel used by a New England woman before the Civil War. In almost perfect condition, the wheel had mellowed to a warm molasses brown, the deep patina of the wood little scarred by time. Sara could imagine herself using it to produce a continuous strand of soft wool twisted from loose fibers, an image so vivid she could almost feel the yarn under her fingers. Her great-aunt was a master weaver, still dyeing her textiles from natural sources: red from pokeberry, orange from bittersweet, yellow from onion skin, and green from goldenrod blossoms. She'd promised to teach Sara to spin, an art she'd mastered as a young woman, if Sara could find a wheel to replace the bundle of worn-out parts used by their female ancestors.

For a moment her view of the spinning wheel was blocked; a tall dark-haired man was examining it with a thoroughness that made Sara nervous. She'd fervently hoped that the lateness of the season would keep away outside dealers, professionals who invariably bid astronomical prices by local standards for fine antiques. The auction had been scheduled on short notice and poorly advertised, apparently because a distant heir was anxious for a cash settlement.

Mentally she tablulated her resources: her twenty-seventh birthday check sent by her parents from Clark Air Force Base in the Philippines, a small sum saved from six months' work as a teller at the Banbury Bank, and the revenue from a government savings bond that had been a high school graduation gift from her godparents. Since most of her savings had gone to purchase her house, it was all she could spare. The total was wholly inadequate to purchase a fine antique spinning wheel at a retail price, but she had high hopes for this auction offering.

The potential bidder was stooping now, examining the legs with far more than amateur keenness. Even a heavy sheepskin-lined coat didn't hide his well-proportioned build, and he certainly wasn't one of the local dairy farmers or horse raisers. She could recognize most of them by now. He stood then, surveying the crowd with calculating interest, undoubtedly doing exactly what Sara had done: sizing up the competition. His eyes rested fleetingly on her face, then swept over the gathering. The hint of a smile showed that he was satisfied with what he saw, but his eyes wandered back to her, studying her face with open curiosity.

Feeling unaccountably flustered, Sara turned away and pretended to read a copy of the auction notice she'd tucked in her shoulder bag. Having grown up on air force bases, she was practically immune to male scrutiny, knowing that her sun-streaked blond hair and sharply defined features were attractive enough, but not outstanding. Her best asset, if she wanted to admit it, was her figure: her small waist, full, firmly molded breasts, and long, well-exercised legs that pushed her height to nearly five feet ten. Today her contours were well concealed under a navy and white ski jacket that did little for her besides providing warmth, and she certainly wasn't expecting anyone at the auction to be appraising her.

No, the stranger's concentration on her had to be sheer calculation, the measuring up of a potential rival. How he'd read her interest in the spinning wheel, she wasn't sure. Perhaps she'd betrayed her alarm by watching too closely while he examined it. Whatever the reason, he definitely had his eyes on her, and he worried her more than a little.

The auctioneer calling the bids was a florid-faced man who seemed determined to extract the last dollar out of the crowd on every lot. He took an interminable amount of time selling an assortment of baskets, refusing to be hurried along when bidding was sluggish.

The tall man had moved away from the spinning wheel and was looking at a pie safe sitting to the rear of the platform, but he didn't fool Sara. His interest in the other piece was feigned, a ploy to take attention from his obsession with the spinning wheel. He was there to buy that one piece; Sara would stake her reputation as a seasoned auction-goer and people-watcher on it.

For a minute she had the advantage, able to stare at him unobserved. In any other situation she would have found him attractive, but as a competitor he had the ruthlessness

13

of Blackbeard stamped on rugged features still bearing traces of a deep summer tan. His eyes were emphasized by dark brows, his cheekbones were high, and his nose just managed not to be too large. His mouth was wide, but drawn into a scowl that made Sara even more apprehensive. He looked like a man who wouldn't allow anyone to outbid him.

A vast number of linens and antique garments were piled on a table, and Sara was afraid the auctioneer would insist on selling them before furniture and larger items were offered. She was pleasantly surprised when the red-faced auctioneer gave up the gavel to his partner after a whispered conference. Apparently they were going to sell the more important lots before the frigid temperature in the barn thinned the crowd.

A Victorian parlor set went at a bargain price, and Sara's hopes soared until she looked at the man she had pinpointed as her enemy. Total indifference was stamped on his face until the spinning wheel was carried to the front of the platform. Needing no encouragement as she readied her bidding paddle for action, Sara held her breath while the auctioneer praised it. Too eager to play it cool and let others begin the bidding, she jumped in on the first call. She soon became aware that her opponents were a heavyset man in overalls and a middle-aged yellow-haired woman just to her left. The auctioneer kept the three of them going until the man dropped out, and Sara sensed rather than heard that the woman's bids were coming with more hesitation. Her heart was singing when, after a long pause, the woman refused to be coaxed into raising the bid one more time.

"Going once . . ."

The voice that topped Sara's bid startled the whole crowd into complete attentiveness, sensing as it did that a real contest was under way. Furious that the dark-haired man had been hanging back, letting her forget about him, Sara quickly made another raise, knowing it had to be her next-to-the-last bid. There was a long silence, the auctioneer obviously expecting the new bidder to make another raise. Then he began his coaxing chant again.

Taking his time, playing with the auctioneer, the man made his raise. With sinking dread, Sara knew she was finished, but she threw in her final bid anyway; if he wanted her spinning wheel, he'd pay as much as she could force him to pay. Unfortunately he was still getting a tremendous bargain.

Sara watched, tight-lipped, as the winner lifted the spinning wheel off the platform with the help of a local farmer who hired his truck for hauling auction purchases. The bidder had been so sure of winning he'd even arranged for trucking! The only good thing about the day was that he seemed to be leaving; she wouldn't have to see the smug satisfaction on his face.

Her first instinct was to leave, maybe to drown her disappointment in a cherry soda at the Main Street Drugstore or to take out a good mystery at the town library. Her bargain hunter's nature got the best of her, though, as the auctioneer turned his attention to the table of fabric items. The lacy curtains in her bedroom were veterans of countless washdays, and she wanted a coarser fabric to highlight the wide pine floorboards. She might be able to pick up some cloth or old curtains for practically nothing and salvage something from the time she'd spent at the auction.

A mountain of worn bed linens and towels had been all but stolen by thrifty Vermonters when something did catch her eye: an antique paisley shawl, a generous square of fine wool with the fringe still intact. The red had faded almost to rose, and the blue was muted by age; but Sara fell in love with it. After losing her coveted spinning wheel, she could at least buy herself a birthday present, assuming it went for a reasonable amount. She didn't want to spend a great deal, however; there would be auctions again in the spring, and one just might offer another spin-

15

ning wheel. Following her most rigid auction rule, she set her limit before the bidding began, optimistic that it would be enough to win the shawl.

Bidding began slowly at the ridiculously low price of five dollars, making Sara even more confident. If the auctioneer didn't recognize the fine antique shawl as a real treasure, her chances were good. She reckoned without the yellow-haired woman, who waved her paddle excitedly, competing more aggressively than she had for the spinning wheel. Disappointed again, Sara dropped out at her self-imposed limit, suspecting that the woman was a sharp dealer or collector in spite of her outdated lavender polyester slacks and quilted nylon coat.

Unexpectedly there was still a contest for the paisley, and searching the crowd for the bidder, Sara was incensed to see that her opponent, the pirate, had returned just in time to buy the shawl. In an auction with hundreds of items, he'd added insult to injury by buying the two items she'd wanted. Her day was ruined, and there was no reason to stay. It would take more than a sweet treat to wash away the bitter taste of having been twice bested. She'd been outbid many times, of course, since auctions were her favorite sport, but never had she felt so angry at being a loser. Maybe it was the self-satisfied smile on the winner's face that got to her.

After returning her bidding paddle to the auction clerk, she zipped her jacket and tossed her navy and yellow scarf around her neck. The barn doors were shut to keep out the worst of the blustery wind, and she exited by a small side door, closing it quickly to spare the remaining auction goers a blast of icy air. She'd never spent a winter in Vermont, but November was making threats; she'd soon have a real sample of New England's roughest season.

Her car was parked far down the road, positioned, she had hoped, for a trouble-free retreat down a hilly, unpaved road. The bleak sky and outdoor solitude were lonely in a way, but they also made her proud of her mother's rugged New England heritage. Her people had been Yankee-bred for more generations than anyone had bothered to trace, and Sara wondered what her life would have been if her mother had settled for a firmly rooted local man instead of her nomadic air force father.

After having attended ten schools in three countries, Sara had spent four secure, marvelous years at a midwestern university, where she majored in hotel and restaurant management. As a career choice it had been a promising field. She'd easily found a job as a management trainee for a large restaurant chain and begun to move up the ladder. What she hadn't considered was that success meant living the same kind of life her parents did, moving to accept new challenges, not daring to refuse new assignments for fear of ruining her chances for advancement. Moving alone to new cities hadn't been a totally satisfying life, but if she hadn't met Bill, she might still be doing it.

Bill Davis came into her life on a quick Christmas trip to see her parents in Texas; she'd used her vacation time for the visit, anticipating that her dad's upcoming assignment in the Philippines might take her parents away for quite a while. She'd always vowed never to become involved with a career air force man, but Bill's flashing blue eyes and quick sense of humor got inside her defenses. Six weeks later they were engaged, and the struggle began, her fiancé demanding that she give up her job immediately and follow him to Germany.

Thinking about their quarrels still depressed her. He'd made her feel selfish, self-centered, but she hadn't been able to throw away everything she valued to live an idle, purposeless life as a military hanger-on. For a while her mother seemed to take Sara's rejection of Bill as a criticism of her own marriage, but at last mother and daughter talked and reached a closer understanding than ever before.

The real casualty of her stormy engagement was her career. Refusing Bill had been the hardest thing she'd ever done, but by the time this happened she had known that a wandering life wasn't for her. She wanted a permanent home, a little white house with green shutters, where her children and grandchildren could visit for years and years, not a series of jerry-built ranch houses or look-alike city apartments. Her life had been filled with here-today, gone-tomorrow friends. She wanted to belong someplace.

Banbury hadn't been a random choice. Her mother's family had once lived throughout the valley, but only her mother's aunt Rachel remained, living in her ancestors' home in the small town. Bill had furiously predicted Sara wouldn't last six months in a town too tiny to have a movie theater, but her mother had been supportive. Six months later Sara knew the decision to live there had been right for her.

Aunt Rachel was a typical New England spinster, if there was such a person in the twentieth century, and Sara adored her. Her aunt's way of life was uncomplicated but certainly not empty; she cared deeply for her friends and neighbors, her town, and her teaching job.

Social life for Sara was no problem; in her job as a bank teller she met everyone in the area, and there was a good chance her boss, Roger Ferris, might become important to her. They worked together and saw each other socially several times a week, and their friendship was growing. In the placid, unhurried atmosphere of Banbury, courting was a leisurely process, pleasant and undemanding. Sara had time, plenty of time, before making a commitment.

Had she parked this far down the road? Daydreaming as she was, could she have walked past her own blue compact? No, it was right ahead, wedged tightly between a pickup truck and, surprisingly, a sleek new Ford EXP, the bumper of the sports car nearly touching hers.

Neither the truck nor the car had been there when she'd parked in a clear stretch, and between them they held her car prisoner. Both vehicles were so close to hers that she had absolutely no room to maneuver, and a ditch beside the road dropped off sharply. She couldn't possibly drive away unless one of the vehicles moved first.

"Great!" she said aloud. "What kind of idiot parks bumper to bumper on a country road?"

"This kind, I'm afraid. Parking was tight when I got here, and I was running late."

"Oh!" She jumped at the unexpected voice.

"Sorry if I startled you," the new owner of the spinning wheel said. "I thought you heard me walking behind you."

"No, I didn't," she said, uncharacteristically confused by the closeness of the man who'd ruined her day.

Maybe she needed glasses! From a distance she'd noticed that he was pleasingly tall and well built, but his air of self-assurance had made her think he was older. Tiny laugh lines by his eyes added warmth, not age, to his face, and the maturity of thirty-some years sat easily on his features. His hair was an unusual shade of deepest brown, giving the illusion of blackness from a distance, and she hadn't noticed the way his dark eyes dominated his other features, as strongly chiseled as they were. It took her a moment to remember how angry she was.

"You have me trapped," she accused him.

"That makes it my lucky day."

"It certainly is," she said, thinking of his winning bid. "The spinning wheel was quite a buy."

"Ah, you recognize me."

"You're carrying a banner," she said, pointing to the shawl folded over his arm, unwilling to have him think she'd particularly noticed his appearance.

"That's why I followed you." He shook it out to let her feast her eyes on the intricate pattern.

"I bid my limit. I couldn't possibly offer you a profit," she said, knowing that merchandise sometimes changed hands at an auction after the winner claimed it.

"No." He laughed at her assumption. "I'm not a dealer looking for a fast sale. I bought this for you."

"For me? You bid against me."

"Not on the shawl. I outbid your competitor after you dropped out."

"I don't understand."

Feeling increasingly awkward, she backed away a step. The steel of the car fender pressed against her hip. There was no one in sight in either direction, and she tried to convince herself that there was no reason to feel threatened by this man. He certainly was friendly now that the bidding was behind them, but he wasn't a person to put others at ease. His coat was unbuttoned in spite of the cold, and she realized his slenderness was partly illusion. His chest was broad and muscular under an expanse of cotton plaid shirt, and his erect stance was a drill instructor's dream.

"The shawl is a gift for you."

Beware of Greeks bearing gifts, she thought, mildly panicked by his offer. She wasn't a woman who accepted gifts from complete strangers, and the shawl had sold for a stiff price.

"I can't accept it," she said weakly, then realized she should have spoken more firmly.

"Of course, you can. It's my apology for pirating your spinning wheel. I could see how much you wanted it."

She was startled by his reference to piracy, especially since she'd gone so far as to imagine him with a black patch over one eye and a cutlass at his waist.

"Then why didn't you let me buy it?" she asked.

"My client has been demanding one all summer; this is the first I've found that meets her requirements."

Somehow Sara wasn't surprised to hear that there was a woman in the picture. This man would always be involved with females, she suspected.

The shawl was in his outstretched hands, but she shook her head and moved a step farther away, leaving the support of the fender to put distance between them.

"I can't possibly accept it. I don't know you."

"I'm Jason Marsh."

"Telling me your name doesn't change anything. Please, I need to leave."

He was blocking her door on the driver's side, and she contemplated scrambling around to the passenger side, but rejected this as unpractical since she might fall into the ditch in the process.

"Telling me yours might."

"If you'll move your car, I'll leave now," she said, ignoring his suggestion that she introduce herself.

He smiled broadly, looking as though he'd just scored a victory, a reaction that totally puzzled her.

"Don't be afraid of me. I'm not the kind of man you meet in dark alleys."

He stepped behind her and draped the shawl over the slippery nylon of her jacket.

"It could have been designed for you," he said with satisfaction, not letting go of it, arranging it on her shoulders. "A woman has to be tall and slender to avoid looking dumpy in a shawl."

"Please don't," she said emphatically, pulling away and leaving the shawl in his hands.

"All right. I'll put it in your car for you."

"No!" She protested too loudly, but her refusal seemed only to amuse him.

"Ah, Yankee stubbornness," he said pleasantly. "I should have anticipated it."

Pleased at having been taken for a native even though she lacked the local twang in her speech, she didn't bother to correct him.

"I thought that auctioneer was going to sell broken rakes until midnight. Did you try the hot dogs at that concession wagon?" he asked.

"No."

"Neither did I. They looked a little green to me. Now I'm starved. Would you like to have lunch with me?" He didn't seem to let her pointed silence discourage him.

"No, thank you."

Exasperated as she was, she was a little tempted by his warm smile. Still, it wasn't her style to go off with strange men, especially not with the man who'd deprived her of her spinning wheel.

"Let me put it this way," he said. "Would you like to meet me at a restaurant, or shall I follow you home?"

"Can't you recognize rejection when you see it?" she asked, torn between amusement and anger at his heavy-handed attempt to pick her up.

"I'm confident your curiosity will win out. You can't figure out a stranger who bought you a gift as compensation for losing an auction battle. A good fisherman always gives a lot of thought to his bait."

"Well, this fish is going home. If you won't move your car, I'll go back to the barn and have the truck owner paged."

"I suppose I should ask if you live alone."

"No, you shouldn't," she snapped, "but I'm well chaperoned by my great-aunt."

He didn't need to know that Aunt Rachel lived three blocks away.

His smile did wonderful things to his face, and he seemed to know how to use it as a weapon.

"I'll look forward to meeting her. Older women always like me. Where do you live? I'm sure I can follow close enough, but you might be more comfortable driving if I don't tailgate. Where are we going?"

"Boston!" she said impatiently.

"With Vermont plates?"

His laughter seemed to fill the countryside, enticing a faint answering smile in spite of her intention to get rid of him.

"If I meet you for lunch, will you promise not to follow me home?" she asked, deciding that she'd better strike the best bargain she could. She was beginning to feel ridiculous, verbally fencing with an overbearing stranger in the middle of the countryside.

"Agreed," he said solemnly, finally moving away from her car door.

She drove intentionally in the opposite direction from Banbury, some internal alarm system warning her that Jason Marsh wasn't like the inexperienced airmen she'd dated so frequently, young men easily put off when they got amorous. There was no harm in lunch, she supposed, although it was almost too late in the afternoon to bother. In a couple of hours she'd be getting ready for her dinner date with Roger.

She drove to a country inn, closely followed by the burgundy EXP. Sibley's Tavern was a favorite restaurant with the summer people in the area, but it closed from December to April. Housed in a long, rectangular wooden building restored to its early-nineteenth-century appearance, the inn was nearly empty of diners at this early hour.

"You picked my favorite restaurant in Vermont," Jason said with a pleased smile as he followed her inside. "Those handwrought iron hinges on the door are original, you know."

She didn't know, but she was becoming more and more curious about this man.

"I've never had dinner with a nameless woman," he said teasingly after a matronly waitress in a long dress had left them with menus.

"This is lunch, and I do have to hurry. I have a dinner date."

And you're making me extremely nervous, she wanted to add, excusing her lack of graciousness as a reaction to his high-handed tactics.

"I'll have the New England boiled dinner, and you'll have what, Miss . . . ?"

He raised one eyebrow, managing to look menacing and teasing at the same time.

"Gilman, Sara," she said, telling him her name as though giving away part of herself.

23

"Well, Gilman, Sara, they make a great home-style horseradish if the roast beef appeals to you."

"I'll have a cup of chowder."

"And?"

"And nothing, thank you. Who are you really?"

He gave their order to the attentive waitress before answering Sara's question.

"Who am I really?" He smiled broadly, and she pretended to be studying a very ordinary salt shaker. "I'm male, as you may have noticed, age thirty-four, single, unattached, though I did have a brief fling at marriage right after college, childless, an excellent bridge player, and a better golfer. Not modest about what I do well. I'm also a bear in the morning, and I like to stay up all night, eating popcorn, listening to jazz, and doing other things."

She laughed at his snappy presentation of facts, forgetting for a moment her intention to be cool and reserved.

"I have two sisters blessedly wed and living on the West Coast, parents retired in Florida, and a cabin in northern Michigan that I haven't had time to use in eighteen months."

"Do you always come on so strong?" she asked.

"Actually, no. I guess I'm riding a high. I've been trying to run down the right spinning wheel all summer. Now I can finish my job in time for some skiing before I have to move on."

"Do you have a job that makes you move often?"

"Pretty often."

"That's a shame."

"I didn't realize you'd miss me when I'm gone," he said, teasing her.

"That's not at all what I meant," she protested quickly. "You just miss so much when you move a lot. The people around you are always strangers. You never have permanent friends."

"You sound like you've done some moving yourself," he said sympathetically.

"That's what my family does best," she said wistfully. "Right now my father's stationed on an air base in the Philippines, and my brother is with the navy in Hawaii. I've never even seen my little nephew."

"Afraid I can't compete when it comes to exotic places. I go to Ohio next."

"To do what?"

"I'm an architect, but basically I restore old buildings. I've been working on an early-nineteenth-century house in Stafford for nearly a year, but I should wrap it up before Christmas. My jobs can take anywhere from six months to several years, although there's always the possibility of something bigger coming along."

"That's a terrible way to live. You can't have a home, a family."

She bit her lip quickly, realizing that she'd said too much to this aggressive stranger.

"I love my work," he said, completely sincere now, "and I've never been any place I didn't enjoy. If your family is military, you must have seen a lot of the world yourself."

"Too much!" she said heatedly. "One year I went to three schools, and my longest time in one school was two and a half years. I was always moving, always giving up friends. I'll never live that way again!"

"So you've come to roost with an old maid aunt," he said critically.

"Old maid is a card game."

"My apologies to your aunt."

His gaze was so piercing she mentally squirmed. Why was she so uncomfortable when he was the one who was pushy, practically forcing her to eat with him?

Their food came, his a hearty full-course dinner and hers a serving of rich chowder. She took tiny sips from her spoon, trying to make it last as long as possible even though she was famished. With this man she needed a focus for her attention, and her soup was the only thing handy. At least she wasn't bored. They talked auctions, and he was an exceptionally keen antiques buff, having an amazing grasp of the market. What was only a hobby to her seemed to be his passion.

"You must have quite a collection of antiques," she said.

"A few at the cabin, if thieves haven't zipped in on their snowmobiles and ripped them off. But I usually just buy for my clients to give my restorations the right furnishings. I don't haul much around with me, mostly clothes and books is all."

"Like a gypsy," she said, remembering that her mother had used the fanciful image of gypsy wagons to sugarcoat a particularly hard move.

"My Romany blood runs thin, but I do tell fortunes," he said, taking her palm in his hand but looking at her eyes, not at her lifeline.

"Clever of you," she said, trying to withdraw her hand without making an issue of it.

His fingers were hard, and his palm was calloused against the softness of her hand; but he kept her fingers in his grip without squeezing them unduly. She hadn't realized her hands were still cold from the frigid air in the barn until she felt the warmth of his.

Heat seemed to radiate from him, surging into her until she was sure her cheeks were flaming pink. He made her feel the same way she had felt when Colonel Wolcott's son kissed her underwater in the swimming pool; only then she'd been fourteen.

Giving herself a mental shake, she tried to match his level stare, sure she was much too old for instant crushes.

"Ah, yes, I see a man in your future, your immediate future. Tomorrow night, I think it is."

"No, it couldn't be tomorrow," she said, succeeding in wrenching her hand from his grasp. "I have a commitment."

26

"Commitment is a high-powered word. I use it only for legal contracts."

"Then I'll just say I'm busy."

"Monday I'll be in New York," he said, talking more to himself than her. "Well, we'll see."

The chime of a tall clock—Sara still preferred to call it a grandfather—reminded her that her objective was to get away quickly.

"Thank you for the chowder," she said, rising from the Windsor-style chair so abruptly she nearly toppled it.

"My pleasure." He smiled, standing also. "Wait until I get the check. I'll walk you to your car."

"No, thank you. Don't trouble yourself. I really have to rush, or I'll be late."

She left hurriedly, but it wasn't her date with Roger that made her rush from the restaurant. Jason Marsh was an unexpectedly congenial dining companion, but the current that had passed between them when he took her hand had filled her with uneasiness. The intensity of his stare as she left had made her drop her eyes, robbing her of the self-assurance that had driven her to top his bids to the limit of her resources. She didn't want to feel so drawn to a gypsy-pirate who'd be gone in a month or so. Falling for a traveling man wasn't for her.

Driving home, she felt like a monkey who'd just escaped the tiger's jaws, shaken, but silly for having put even one toe in its territory.

Her street of small white-sided houses, built generations ago in uncomplicated Vermont box shapes, wasn't as attractive now as when the giant maples had their foliage, but Sara eagerly awaited the fluffy white frosting that the first winter snow would bring. This was where she belonged, a place where her ancestors had thrived. Jason Marsh was a terrific hunk of man, to put it bluntly, but she owed it to herself to forget him.

Why did she expect this to be difficult? After all, the man hadn't even asked for her address.

27

## CHAPTER TWO

The ring was shrill, deliberately set at the loudest level because Sara had decided to economize and make do with a single phone on her bedside stand. To hear it in the kitchen, she needed maximum volume, but when she was right beside it, she jumped every time.

"Sara, dear," her great-aunt said, getting to her objective without preliminaries, "I'm afraid your bank has my checking account a bit confused again. Could you take a look at it for me?"

"I'll be glad to," Sara answered, trying not to feel disappointed because her caller was Aunt Rachel, making her almost daily check on her favorite niece's child. "Do they show your balance short or over?"

"Short. I checked it with that little pocket calculator you gave me for my birthday, dear, but there's still a matter of sixteen dollars and two cents."

Sara smiled at her aunt's monthly woe, but her mind was still back at Saturday's auction and Sibley's Tavern. Jason hadn't asked for her phone number; he didn't even know her town, since she'd deliberately misled him into thinking she lived east, not west, of the auction site. He couldn't possibly call her, so she absolutely had to stop feeling letdown every time the phone rang.

"I'm going to the high school band concert tonight, Aunt Rachel, but I'll stop by after work tomorrow and straighten it out."

For more than forty years her great-aunt had guided one class after another of lively first graders through their ABC's and 1, 2, 3's, sometimes knowing her charges better after a few months than their own parents did, but the procedure for keeping her checkbook balanced escaped her. Sara was sure her great-aunt had an advanced case of math anxiety when it came to finances, but she willingly did this small monthly favor, relieving the bank's president, an old school friend of her aunt's, of the chore.

Aunt Rachel might be a little foggy on figures, but she did know old houses, avidly visiting them every summer.

On impulse Sara asked, "Are any important houses in the county being restored this year, Aunt Rachel?"

"Well, let me think. Beaver Run Inn isn't a private home anymore, but I've heard they mean to do some work on it. Would you like to see it? My friend Alvina is second cousin to the committee chairperson in charge of the museum. I'm sure I could arrange a guided tour for you."

"Oh, no, that won't be necessary. I just met an architect last weekend who said he's working on a house in Stafford. I wondered if you know which one it is."

"Don't tell me you met Jason Marsh!"

"Why . . . yes. How did you know?"

"The Attwaters were so fortunate to get him. He did the General John Dana house. You must have seen the article about it in one of my antiques magazines, just pages and pages of colored pictures showing his wonderful work. I must look it up for you."

"I didn't realize I was meeting a celebrity," she said wryly. "He's the man who bought my spinning wheel."

"Oh, Sara, meeting Jason Marsh is well worth a spinning wheel. There are lots of spinning wheels, but Mr.

Marsh is absolutely number one in his field. He doesn't just do dull things like fixing roofs and repairing foundations. He re-creates the past, right down to the smallest detail. If he bought the spinning wheel, it's because it belongs in the Attwater house."

"Aunt Rachel! You were going to teach me to spin."

"Oh, and I will, dear, but imagine, meeting Jason Marsh. Did you talk to him?"

"A little, but I don't think I'll be seeing him again."

"That's a shame. I would love to know how he salvaged the leather wall covering in the Dana parlor. People sometimes used leather instead of paper or fabric, you know."

"Yes, but I have to run, Aunt Rachel. Roger's picking me up. His niece is playing in the concert. I'll see about your checkbook tomorrow."

Sara wrote a quick note to herself so she wouldn't forget to stop at her great-aunt's, but her mind was on Jason Marsh. Even though Aunt Rachel was a restoration buff, it was still surprising that she knew his name. Her great-aunt subscribed to almost every publication covering the antiques and restoration fields, studying them religiously from cover to cover, but she couldn't possibly remember every name she read. Jason's work had really impressed her.

School concerts began inconveniently early, Sara decided as she hurried to run water in the tub, pinning her long blond hair on her head to keep it dry. Much as she loved a leisurely soak in her huge claw-footed tub, a quick rinse would have to suffice. Roger was a fanatic when it came to being on time; she could never depend on him for so much as five extra minutes to get ready.

She was still sitting in front of her dressing table mirror, wearing only bra and panties, when her doorbell sounded. Being on time was one thing, but Roger was nearly twenty minutes early, she thought with a twinge of irritation. He knew she'd left the bank later than usual.

After finishing her lips and blotting her lipstick, she slipped into her quilted red robe and hurried to the door.

"Hello. Remember me?"

"Why, yes, of course," she said, stammering in her mind, if not actually doing it aloud. "Mr. Marsh, the man with my spinning wheel."

"May I come in?"

"The truth is," she said, stepping aside to let him enter, "I'm expecting someone else."

"Are you ready for him, or are you rushing to get ready?" he asked with a cynical smile.

"Obviously I'm not ready for a high school band concert, which is where we're going," she snapped.

"I can top that bid," he said. "Dinner at the Sibley's Tavern and a guided tour of the house I'm restoring."

"I can't break an appointment at a moment's notice to go out with you," she said, genuinely rattled that he would expect her to do so.

"An appointment! Here I worried that you might have a date."

"It is a date. With one of my bosses. A vice-president at the bank."

She flushed, realizing how silly she must sound, trying to impress Jason Marsh with the importance of her date. He must think she was an absolute bumpkin, and that didn't please her at all.

"The vice-president is taking you to a high school concert?"

His question was innocent enough, but the laugh lines beside his eyes deepened, making him look roguish.

"His niece plays first clarinet."

"That explains it. Shall I tell him you've changed your mind when he comes?"

"No, you shall not! I'm not going to break my date with Roger. If you wanted me to go out, you should have called first."

Her eyes narrowed suspiciously as she remembered that

he couldn't call her; he wasn't even supposed to know the town where she lived.

"How did you find me?"

"Don't you know?" His brows arched mischievously. "Like the stallion finds the mare."

"I think you'd better leave."

"I'm sorry," he said, instantly looking contrite.

"Instead of apologizing, tell me how you found me."

"When you left the auction barn, I paid my bill and managed to distract the clerk long enough to read your registration."

Of course! Auctions always required a driver's license or other identification before issuing a number. Her name and address were on the registration sheet beside her number, which he could easily have read on her bidding paddle.

"You knew my name before you followed me!"

"Guilty, I'm afraid."

"And where I lived!"

"Actually I didn't get your street number, but I stopped at a pay phone by the gas station and used its directory, Gilman, Sara. You should list your phone number under S. Gilman to discourage creeps who prey on single women."

"In this town it's not necessary. This is a safe, sane place to live."

"I hope so, Gilman, Sara."

He slipped off his heavy suede coat, the same one he'd worn to the auction, and dropped it casually on a rocker near the door.

"You can't stay," she protested, not at all sure how Roger would react to finding another man in her living room. He was used to a clear field.

"I'll just watch some TV, have a few beers if you have them. I don't mind waiting until the concert's over. I told you, I'm a night person."

"Please, Mr. Marsh—"

"Jason," he interrupted. "I thought we'd progressed to first names."

"All right. Jason. I have other plans tonight. You can't wait here."

"My business in New York took a couple of days instead of one," he said conversationally, ignoring her appeal for him to leave, walking to her fireplace, and laying a birch log on the cold grate. "In fact, I just got back, and I'm starved. Do you want me to whip up some dinner for the two of us? Let's see, when does the concert start?"

"Seven thirty, but—"

"Should be over by nine. It must be a pretty small high school."

"It's a consolidated district, but that has nothing to do with your staying here."

He stood suddenly and moved so close to her that the faint spicy fragrance of his after-shave was detectable. Almost against her will, she met his eyes, as dark as ebony with glints of amber gold. She couldn't help blinking first; the intensity of his gaze made her feel insecure.

"Some people," he said softly, "become very uneasy when another person invades what they consider their space. You aren't one of them, are you?"

She was about to back away from him, but she forced herself to stand her ground.

"It's a favorite experiment of mine to see how close another person will let me come."

"Really, this is pointless," she protested.

Still, not only was he invading her space, but he'd eliminated it. Their bodies were separated by a hairline crack of air, and his face was so close it was out of focus. When his lips brushed hers, it was like her first kiss all over again, strange and a little threatening. His lips were dry and firm, massaging hers gently until they parted slightly. Expecting him to press his advantage, she felt deserted when he moved away.

33

"You really do have a date on his way?" he asked hoarsely.

"Yes, really."

"Then this will have to last."

He scooped her into his arms, kissing her forcefully but quickly.

"Would it be easier for you if I left now?" he whispered regretfully.

"Yes."

"I will, but there's a price."

"What?" she asked, trying to force her mind back to the practical complications of having two men in her living room at the same time.

"Tomorrow night. A mystery trip with me."

"A mystery trip?"

"That means you trust me to plan the evening. Count on me for dinner; the rest will be a surprise."

From the mantel her old wooden Sears, Roebuck clock chimed seven times with more volume than melody. It gained at least five minutes a day, but she'd wound and reset it the day before. Roger would be there within minutes; he always allowed at least half an hour, even though the high school was only ten minutes away.

"Your clock is a little fast," Jason said in a tone meant to reassure her.

"Oh, all right. Leave now, and I'll see you tomorrow."

"Can you be ready by seven?"

"Yes, but only if you go right now."

For a moment she was sure he'd kiss her again, but he only smiled.

"See you then."

He put on his coat on the way out the door, turning around for only an instant to flash a smile at her.

When he was gone, she pressed her lips with two fingers, imagining that his kiss had left them hot to the touch. The man was impossible; he barged in without warning and went to any means to get what he wanted. Her decision at the tavern not to let anything develop between them had been the right one; he could only confuse and complicate her life. If she felt a little breathless, it was only because she was in a rush to dress. Jason Marsh was aggressive to the point of being overbearing, and that macho technique didn't work with her.

The front door flew inward before she left the spot where he'd kissed her.

"I didn't meet your aunt," Jason called out to her.

For a moment Sara forgot that she'd implied Aunt Rachel lived with her.

"Is she here?" He walked into the front room, looking around as if he expected to find her aunt hiding behind the sofa. "She's not here, is she?"

"Why do you say that?"

"This room is all yours, warm honey brown, bittersweet, pale fawn. If she lived here, she'd leave some imprint on the place. Am I right? Never mind, I know I am. Homes are my business."

He took her lack of denial as assent, disappearing as suddenly as he'd burst into the room, reminding her that she needed a lock that worked automatically.

A vein was pulsing in her forehead, and she could feel her heart beating. Having hurried to her bedroom mirror, she was startled by her appearance. Her lips were swollen, her eyes looked glazed, and her expression was that of a woman in shock. Jason Marsh had no right to explode into her life and destroy her composure. He'd blackmailed her into agreeing first to lunch Saturday and now to an evening together. If Roger hadn't been on his way, she would have put Jason out of her life once and for all. As it was, she'd have to call him and cancel. She wasn't going to risk her emotional equilibrium in another head-on collision with that man!

Roger! He was at the door, and she was nowhere near ready. After running to let him in, she stumbled through a quick apology and raced to finish dressing.

Still wearing his banker's clothes—an ash gray three-piece suit, white shirt, and charcoal tie—Roger tried to hide his irritation when Sara appeared fifteen minutes later. She was wearing her red wool dress, hoping it would make her look cheerful and account for the flush that hadn't faded from her cheeks. Roger didn't seem to notice anything but the time.

The band was warming up with a squawk of sounds when he managed to locate two empty seats at the rear. They were so far back Roger was forced to put on his glasses, a second point against her since he hated wearing them with a passion.

Sara wasn't sure why he needed to see well at a concert, but she settled back with her own thoughts, most of them centered on her problem with Jason. She would break their date, of course, but she was honest enough to admit it would be hard. Jason's kisses felt so right; they reminded her of Bill's before they had begun quarreling so much, but there was a special quality to Jason's that she couldn't pinpoint. She could still feel the texture of his lips, slightly roughened by cold winds, taste the dried-apple sweetness of his mouth, and remember the tickling of his breath under her nose. As the amateur musicians plugged away at their selections, she remembered the way his lips parted slightly when he smiled at her, wondering what it was about his eyes that made them seem to lighten when he was amused.

"Megan did well in her solo," Roger whispered to Sara.

"Yes," she agreed, embarrassed that she'd completely missed the big moment that had brought the whole Ferris family to the high school auditorium. In fact, she would have been hard pressed to name a single number that the band had played up to then.

"I think John should look into a new clarinet for her, though. She should have a professional-quality instrument if she's going on with her music, and, of course, she is," Roger went on.

In his family decisions were usually joint affairs, and although Roger was a bachelor eight years younger than his brother, he took a strong personal interest in the upbringing of his niece and nephew. His sister-in-law, Betty, had confided to Sara that it was high time he had a family of his own to fuss over; her theory was that a man should marry before he was thirty-five, or he couldn't be molded into a proper husband. That made Roger just two years short of hopeless. It also made Jason a borderline case.

With an immense effort of will Sara forced herself to concentrate on the rest of the concert, but Megan's magic moment wasn't repeated. The program ended with a famous march, but she couldn't stop herself from remembering the popular parody of it, one concerning feathered friends and ducks' mothers. As a cultural evening it was something of a bust.

It was a sign of Roger's annoyance at her that they had their late dinner at the Dunbar Café, the only place to eat in town after nine in the evening; in fact, it was the only place for a meal at any time except for the counter in the drugstore, but they often drove to a nearby town to dine.

Roger didn't kiss her good night either; he always kissed her three times at her door; once lightly on her upper lip, once on her forehead, and once more soundly on her mouth. She rather liked the last of the trio, but often she wished he'd vary the pattern a bit. Roger had to be pretty put out to omit his routine.

"It was a nice concert," she said, fibbing.

"Well, I think most of them need to practice more, but Megan did well."

Sara agreed with a nod; not having heard a note of the solo, she couldn't think of a suitable comment.

Something bad was happening, she realized as she got ready for bed; she was comparing Roger to Jason, and that was about as fair as comparing a milk cow to a racehorse. They were different breeds, and of course, Roger wasn't as amusing or dashing as Jason. That was why she liked

37

Roger; he was a comfortable person, reliable, staunch in his beliefs, loyal to his family and community.

In Banbury Roger was considered quite a catch, good-looking in a scrubbed blond way, well established at the bank, and socially secure as a member of a family that traced its lines back to Colonial days. What was important to Sara was that he was also a nice person; if he'd been a bit irritable tonight, it was her fault. She'd almost made him late for a concert that was far more important to him than to her. Roger wasn't crazy about auctions, but he dutifully attended them whenever she asked; she owed him the courtesy of doing the same for activities that interested him.

Accepting the blame for the unsuccessful evening, Sara crawled under her down plaid comforter ready for sleep. With the lights out, the room was a silent cocoon, totally restful, unlike her bedrooms near air bases and busy city streets. Usually she fell asleep almost instantly, but to-night she couldn't find a comfortable position. She flopped from side to side, from stomach to back, but she couldn't turn off the thoughts that were keeping her alert.

In the morning she'd call Jason and cancel their date; she was under no obligation to keep her word when he'd blackmailed her into giving it. True, she was attracted to him; he had the kind of rugged good looks that stimulated fantasies. Not only that, he was tall enough to make her feel dominated, an unusual sensation for a girl of her height. Roger was six feet, a perfectly acceptable height, but her eyes met his when she wore even modestly high heels.

That was the reason Jason impressed her so much, of course. She could look up to him; he made her feel delicate and feminine. The sheer novelty of the sensation was making her butter-brained. What she felt for him was a crazy infatuation; she might as well resist it now instead of becoming involved and getting hurt. The man was leaving in a month, and Banbury was her permanent home. If they became serious about each other, both would suffer. She would be doing him a favor and protecting herself by breaking their date.

The phone shattered her drowsy state, making her sit bolt upright so quickly her heart pounded.

"Hello!"

"You sound startled. Did I wake you?"

Jason's voice was a rich baritone, unmistakable even on the somewhat distorting local line.

"Yes . . . no. I was almost asleep, I guess."

"Sorry, I assumed you'd still be up. You'll never catch me bringing you home this early. You are alone, aren't you?"

"Of course," she said angrily.

His small chuckle made her even madder; he'd never doubted that she was in bed by herself. Now, while she was angry, was the time to break their date.

"About tomorrow night . . ."

"That's why I'm calling. My client is coming in to check the progress on the house and go over some final details. I didn't get her message until I got home this evening, so it's too late to head her off. I'm afraid I won't be done until late."

"Oh, that's okay," she said.

She wouldn't have to use any of her carefully invented excuses after all. The date was canceled, thanks to Jason's client. Her momentary surge of relief was overshadowed by irritation. How far did his obligation to his client extend? Were wining and dining his patron part of his success scheme?

"Would you like me to call you when she leaves, or would Friday night be better?"

"No, don't call," she said too quickly.

"That's probably better. I'll pick you up around seven on Friday."

"Wait," she said, afraid he'd hang up thinking they had a date.

"You're not going to tell me your banker has you booked on Friday?"

"No, but I just don't know if we should start anything. I mean, you'll be leaving soon and . . ."

What she was trying to say wasn't coming out well at all, and his silence didn't help.

"Maybe we should just forget it," she said awkwardly.

The silence on his end of the line seemed to last for aeons. She could hear his sharp intake of breath but couldn't think of anything else to say.

"I'm not going to let you off the hook that easily, Sara." His voice sounded unnaturally strained. "I don't think I can just forget you."

"Maybe you should." Her voice was so low she wondered if he'd heard.

"No, I don't believe that. One way or another, you're going to have to tell me how you really feel face-to-face, or I just won't accept it."

"I am telling you."

"No, the phone is too easy. I'll be there Friday at seven, unless you want me to come there now."

"No, don't do that!"

"I don't know if I can wait until Friday," he said so softly she had to strain to hear. "Well, Friday then," he said in his normal voice. "We don't have to go anywhere if you don't want to. Don't decide now. Tell me when I get there."

Torn between wanting to see him again and fearing the consequences, she meekly assented. At least she'd have plenty of time to rally her resistance. Regardless of how easily the famous Jason Marsh usually got his way, things would be different with her. She wasn't going to be swept up into a relationship that couldn't possibly end happily.

"Go to sleep now, Sara. I'll be thinking of you."

His voice was a caress that sent warm tingles through her body.

"Good night," she said, drained of energy.

The spot where she was lying was too warm, the thick comforter capturing her body heat and stifling her. When she rolled to a fresh spot on her queen-size bed, she shivered, the sheets icy on her feet and legs left exposed as her flannel nightgown rode up. With a great deal of twisting and squirming she drew her gown around her hunched-up knees for a baglike effect, but her restlessness made comfort evasive.

Her conversation with Jason played over and over in her mind, always coming back to his promise that he'd be thinking of her. Well, she was thinking of him, and warning alarms were wailing in her brain. She was terribly afraid this man had the power to tumble her carefully ordered life like a house of cards. Already he'd made her aware of how empty her large bed was.

How would it feel to cuddle spoonlike against his broad back on chilly nights, to know that when she woke, he'd be there to cradle her head on his chest? Just thinking about it stirred sensations she preferred to avoid. She'd run the gauntlet of physical attraction with Bill, emerging scarred but determined to be her own person. Now another trap was poised to spring, and she sensed it was far more dangerous.

"Oh, damn," she said aloud, sitting up to rest her head dejectedly on pulled-up knees.

Why did she have to meet a man without roots just when she'd found a place that satisfied her need for permanence? She loved her life in Banbury, the people she met at the bank, the neighbors who'd welcomed her with steaming casseroles and homemade bread on moving day, and the younger adults who worked in Main Street businesses and stopped to chat in the bank. If Jason could become part of this peaceful, orderly existence, his attentions would be more than welcome.

She certainly wasn't indifferent to the unspoken messages he was sending; because he was self-assured, in command of his own life, the pull of his personality was powerful. He tempted her to put herself in his hands, surrender her independence of mind in return for rewards as yet unpromised. He made her more aware of being female; he touched her breasts just by noticing them from across the room, the look of secret pleasure on his face telling her that he knew the hard-tipped swelling was his doing. When he admired her hair, she felt sultry and alluring, as though she had brushed it until electricity charged through it just so he could touch it.

Hugging her legs even harder, she pressed her chin against the hard knobs of her knees, no longer fighting the urge to fantasize. Until she'd met Roger, she'd never had a satisfying platonic relationship with a man. Her electric blue eyes and full pink mouth had left a trail of infatuated boys since junior high, and because she'd developed early and rather spectacularly, a lot of the wrong kind of attention had come her way too soon. She knew the boys had whispered about her when they drew their bikes in a circle on the way home from school, and later, in high school, she couldn't remain totally unaware of being an object of locker-room speculation.

Because she'd been pressured to respond to boys before she was emotionally ready, she still tended to shy off. When Bill had first swept into her life, she hadn't felt ready for a deep relationship, but the failure still smarted. Now her physical attraction to Jason made her feel fragmented; she needed time for a leisurely courtship, a gradual growing-together process. The last thing she wanted was a headlong dash into another serious romance. She had to have the presence of mind to avoid him before it was too late to back off with her heart intact.

For once she was glad that her job at the bank was mostly undemanding routine. Even then she managed to make a minor error, sleepy and distracted as she was after her restless night. Worse, she compounded her inefficiency by not being able to spot her own mistake in response to a customer's complaint. Finally Roger came over to help her, his exasperated patience worse than a rebuke. He found her slip-up easily and helped her pacify the customer, carefully avoiding any personal comments. In fact, he avoided her most of the day; Sara suspected it was his way of telling her that their evening had been less than successful.

"Thanks for helping me with Mr. Baurer," she said as they left the bank at the same time after closing for the day. "I don't know what got into me today."

"Maybe I shouldn't have made such an issue about being late last night," he said guardedly, grudgingly conceding that he might be the cause of her fuzzy-mindedness at work.

"That's okay, Roger." She wasn't too pleased having him think she was upset because of his irritation, but as a conciliatory gesture she asked, "Would you like to come to my place for dinner? I'm going to pick up some lamb chops on the way home."

"Thanks, but I can't this evening. A few of us are going to Denton for my cousin Margaret's birthday. I would have invited you, of course, but she hasn't been feeling good. The family decided it'd better be a quiet family affair, just a representative from each branch."

"Has she been sick?" Sara asked, but her mind wasn't on Roger's distant relative, an eighty-seven-year-old woman for whom the title of cousin was largely honorary. He started explaining a rather complicated sugar imbalance problem, but her mind was elsewhere.

When Roger left her, she felt mildly relieved that she hadn't been included in the Ferris family gathering. She was tired, and she needed time to decide what to do about Jason. To her great consternation, she was beginning to feel that never seeing him again would be more painful than keeping their date.

On pleasant days she walked to work, enjoying the quiet, tree-shaded streets and unhurried atmosphere of the town, but the morning had been cold and overcast. She'd driven with the intention of doing her grocery shopping on the way home. The modest-sized store that passed as a supermarket in Banbury wasn't crowded on Thursday because most local people shopped after their Friday payday. Country dwellers preferred the traditional Saturday-in-town to get supplies, so Sara had the store almost to herself.

Finally, after six months at the bank, the cashier in the market was beginning to greet her without the frozen politeness reserved for summer people. Sara hadn't yet crossed the line between home folks and outsiders, but with her great-aunt's sponsorship, she was making headway. Different groups had asked her to substitute at bridge or bowling, and the women's auxiliary of a local lodge had extended her a reserved invitation to apply for membership on the basis of her grandfather's long association with the organization before his death. They couldn't guarantee, of course, that no one would cast a black ball against her, but they were optimistic. She declined, with thanks, rejecting the ritual and rigmarole, not the members.

Her phone rang as she was putting the last brown bag of groceries on her scrubbed pine kitchen table. With a guilty start she remembered Aunt Rachel's unbalanced checkbook.

"Aunt Rachel," she began hurriedly as she picked up the receiver, knowing she had to get her say in quickly, "I'll be over in about twenty minutes."

"Lucky Aunt Rachel."

Jason's amusement was contagious, and she laughed at her mistake.

"I promised my aunt I'd balance her checkbook. When she calls, I have to get my two cents in fast, or she's off on something else. She's a fan of yours, by the way."

"A fan?"

"She subscribes to all the antiques magazines. I guess she's read about your work."

44

"You must have mentioned my name to her," he accused her teasingly.

Knowing she'd trapped herself, Sara tried to sound like a good sport.

"How else would I know you're famous?"

"Am I?" He laughed. "Well, I've never been asked for my autograph, but your aunt is welcome to be the first."

"Why are you calling?" she asked with a dim hope that he might be canceling their date. The prospect didn't please her as much as it should have.

"My client is freshening up for dinner. I wanted to hear your voice."

"Well, you've heard it," she said, not pleased, either, by the thought that his client might be some beautiful society woman, rich enough to hire him and idle enough to give his work lots of supervision. "I do have to go find the problem in my aunt's checking account."

"I'll see you tomorrow then."

"Yes."

Once he'd hung up, she wished they'd talked longer, but what was there to say?

Her great-aunt pressed her to stay for dinner, but Sara declined, trying to convince herself it wasn't because Jason might call again.

Tired as she was in the late evening, she kept finding things to do to avoid going to bed. When her household jobs were done, she decided her nails were a disaster and labored over them until her eyelids drooped. Before she crawled into bed, she muted the phone ring, not wanting to be startled awake too abruptly if she did get a late-night call.

The adjustment was unnecessary. The phone didn't ring that night.

## CHAPTER THREE

On Friday Sara toyed with the idea of preparing dinner for Jason at her house, remembering that he'd left their plans up to her, but by the time the bank closed that afternoon she'd rejected an evening at her place as too cozy, preferring to take her chances on his mystery trip.

Twenty minutes before Jason was due, she gave up trying to guess where they might be going and decided to wear her favorite skirt, a lightweight dusky blue wool gathered at the waist by a wide matching belt. With her ivory silk blouse it seemed to strike the right balance between casualness and formality. Her hair, freshly shampooed and blow-dried, gleamed with glints of gold, and she'd taken special care with her makeup, using it sparingly but skillfully. The results didn't displease her, but caring about them did. Her reason told her it was insane to fuss for Jason, but her ego craved the approval of this man, however badly it all ended.

Jason was twenty minutes late, and he didn't bother to apologize. Because Roger's obsession with to-the-minute promptness wasn't his most admirable trait in her eyes, Sara found the architect's tardiness wholly forgivable.

"You look beautiful," Jason said when she opened the door.

"Thank you. Come in."

"I brought some wine."

"That was thoughtful," she said, taking it. "I haven't fixed dinner, though."

"Fine. I just wanted to be prepared either way."

"Would you like some now?"

"No, not unless you would. We can save it for another time."

His sureness that there'd be another time rattled her.

"I could make an omelet or something if you don't want to go out," she offered, forgetting all the hazards of an intimate dinner at home.

"No, I made a dinner reservation in case you wanted to go out."

"I'll get my coat."

Earlier she'd taken her coat from the hall closet and left it on her bed, sensing that she might need a breather before they left. Going for it, she decided their brief conversation had been inane to the point of being asinine. They sounded like two amateur actors in a bad play. She put on her camel-colored wool coat and tied the belt before leaving the room, not wanting Jason Marsh's assistance.

"Ready?" he asked needlessly, and she nodded, hoping their conversation would get down to antiques and auctions soon. These seemed to be the safest subjects and their only common meeting ground.

"I have to confess the mystery trip is off," he said as they drove beyond the outskirts of town. "I canceled the plane because I wasn't sure you'd go."

"Plane! Where were we going?"

"Boston."

"Oh, no!" She laughed then, a hearty outburst that made him smile. "You were going to take me to Boston just for dinner?"

"You're not that naïve, Sara."

47

She wasn't, so she hurriedly switched to another topic.

"I gather you fly planes yourself?"

"I have a pilot's license, yes. Are you glad I canceled out?"

"Of course, I'm glad. I'm not going to spend the weekend with you in Boston."

"I never mentioned a weekend. I thought we'd take it one night at a time."

His tone was light and teasing, but she could read between the lines. If it wasn't his intention to have a fast fling before he left town, then all her experience on air bases crawling with men had been misleading.

"In other words, I'd have to audition," she said, playing along in the same mood. "I haven't done that since I wanted to be the princess in a fourth-grade play."

"Did you win the part?"

"No, I had to be the goose girl. I was the only one in the class who could tower over the short kids who played the geese. The princess was a foot shorter than I was and looked like a porcelain doll."

"Well, better a goose girl than a tree. That's what I played in my theatrical debut. It's hard to get into the spirit of a part when all you do is wave your branches."

"You weren't really a tree?"

"Yes, in Mrs. Peabody's third-grade epic. The tall boys had to be the trees."

"And I thought being tall was an asset for boys."

"For basketball players maybe."

"Did you play?"

"Basketball? No. It's the one sport that never appealed to me. I played football and tennis in high school."

"Why didn't you like basketball?" she asked defensively.

"Floor burns."

"Floor burns?"

"It took a while for my coordination to catch up with my growth, and floor burns hurt a whole lot more than the

48

lumps we took in football. Actually I just wasn't very good at basketball."

"I can't imagine you as a gangly kid. I played basketball in high school."

"Were you good at it?"

"Not great, but I enjoyed it. Until we moved in midseason one year, and I didn't bother going out again."

"You should have. Team sports are a great way to get acquainted."

"It doesn't matter now."

"It shouldn't. Do you ski?"

"I love trying. Maybe I'll improve living in Vermont."

"Only if you get out on the slopes with a good teacher."

"I don't suppose you have anyone in mind."

"Could be."

A few miles out of town he turned right at a crossroad that was unfamiliar to her.

"Are you going to tell me where we're going?"

"Sure. This is a shortcut to Sibley's Tavern."

"Oh, that's nice," she said, and it was. At least they'd be on familiar turf, and the place was sure to be crowded on one of the last Friday nights of its season. Better still, the many antiques on display would give them a rich source of conversation.

Much of the lower floor of the tavern was arranged for dining, but the tables were set up in a series of small rooms, not in a single large one, creating an atmosphere of intimacy that was lacking in most restaurants. Oil-burning lamps flickered on every white-clothed table, and the long ruffled skirts of the waitresses swished as they moved over the bare floorboards. Their table near the fireplace was in what had once been the commons area. The tables and chairs were sturdy reproductions of old tavern furnishings, and a small but safe gas fire now flamed on the open hearth; however, all the decorative pieces were authentic relics of the tavern's heyday, the early 1800s. The firearms hung on the brick chimney

49

could have been left behind by early patrons stopping for a draft of the bitter local brew, and old crockery and pewter mugs sat on wall shelves under rough-hewn beams. The walls were whitewashed stone for nearly four feet, with a rough plaster surface bridging the gap to the ceiling. The only disadvantage was that the ceiling was lower than modern ones, and both Sara and Jason instinctively hunched up a little when they entered the room, which was the oldest and least altered in the building.

In the absence of a cloakroom Jason hung their coats on hooks embedded in one wall, then smoothly sat her at their table for two. He was more polished than personal as he requested cocktails, discussed the menu with her, and placed his order for lobster and hers for a seafood platter that included a lobster tail.

"Sure you don't want the whole lobster?" he said, double-checking, but she declined, preferring to sample a variety.

"This is a great place to visit now," she said, surveying the room, "but I wouldn't like to have lived in it when it was new."

"I'm sure you wouldn't," he said, smiling. "A woman living alone then was an oddity. Her neighbors might think she was a witch if she could survive on her own."

"Witches were useful people. They knew about herbs and cures, and their neighbors went to them the way they would a doctor."

"And for recreation they went flying on their brooms."

"Well, I'd rather be the village witch than be married to some brute who kept me under his thumb."

"No man could keep you under his thumb unless you wanted to be tied down," he said, laughing.

"Look at that strange object hanging to your left," she said, pointing.

Barely glancing away from her, he said, "Tongs used to light a pipe with a hot coal. It has a built-in tamper."

"I think that piece would stump even Aunt Rachel."

"Did you know your aunt well before you moved here?"

"Not really. She's an avid correspondent, though, so even before I could scribble little notes to her, she sent me comic postcards and letters on scented stationery. I always knew I had a great-aunt, even though we saw her only once in a while."

"My sister Judy is like that, always writing up a storm, but Joanie thinks stationery was invented to make grocery lists."

"Do you see your sisters often?"

"Not as often as I'd like. I have three nephews and a niece, ages three to twelve. I'd like to have the boys at the cabin for a while next summer. Get to know them before they're grown-up."

"And not your niece?"

"She's the three-year-old. I'll pass on her until she's a little older, even if that makes me a chauvinist."

"I didn't say you were."

"Didn't you?" He arched his brows in the way that transformed him into the ruthless pirate, throwing out a challenge she chose to ignore.

She quickly changed the subject back to antiques, asking him about a standing salt on a far shelf, even though she could identify it perfectly well herself.

Admit it, Sara, she thought between a bite of scallop and a buttery chunk of lobster tail, you're not interested in him because he knows antiques. Jason Marsh could talk about pipes and plungers, and you'd be fascinated.

"Did you study antiques in college?" she asked. "I've heard some universities are offering courses in the fine arts curriculum."

"No, I studied architecture, and I'm not going to say another word about antiques," he said abruptly, pulling off the paper bib furnished with his lobster.

"Why not?" She was genuinely surprised at his sudden change from urbane conversationalist to petulant escort.

"Because you're leading me around the displays in this

51

room by my ego to keep from talking about anything important, you, for instance."

"There isn't anything to say about me."

"What I want to know about you could fill volumes."

He spoke so softly that she had to strain to hear his voice over the hum of dinner conversations and dishes being served and removed. The lamp flame burned low between them, partly obscuring his mouth but illuminating his eyes, deep-set and searching, riveted on her face in a disconcerting way. When she looked down at her hand, nervously folding and refolding her cloth napkin, he reached across the table and tilted her chin lightly upward with one finger, forcing her to look directly at him.

"Don't look away," he said, "or I'll think you're trying to hide some dark secret."

"There are no secrets in my life."

"Your whole life is a mystery to me."

"Not one that even Agatha Christie could have done much with."

"Ah, a mystery reader. I knew you had unsuspected depths. Who's your favorite author?"

"Oh, Agatha, because she fools me time after time. I'm not nearly clever enough for her."

"Neither am I! But I like the thrillers, spies, and chases, things that make my life seem tame."

"Your life is anything but tame! Every job you do is a new challenge, not like working in a bank, where one deposit is just like all the others."

"That's why I stick with it. I've never renovated a building that didn't have special problems of its own. I'm constantly in hot water, trying to figure out how to handle one disaster after another. Once a whole wall collapsed on me because I tried to rush; that mistake cost me a week in the hospital."

"I never thought of your work as dangerous."

"It isn't if I use my head and take reasonable precautions. I'm not fond of roof work, however."

"Acrophobia?"

"No, just a healthy respect for steep inclines and slippery shingles."

"I can understand that. I followed my brother up on a garage roof when I was little. He got down, but I was stuck, too scared to move. I still feel a little guilty because he got the blame, and he'd told me not to do it."

"Typical sister!" he said teasingly. "Mine were monsters at times."

"Well, having an older brother is no lark. Boys are so bossy!"

"Don't you think older sisters are?"

"Maybe it's all older siblings who are a pain in the neck," she said, laughing.

"Undoubtedly. The youngest one always suffers."

"But sometimes we get even!"

"Absolutely! I found frogs and snakes potent weapons."

"I sometimes resorted to blackmail."

"I'll bet you were good at it, but tell me, Sara, how did you end up living in Banbury so far from the rest of your family?"

"My great-aunt—"

"No, don't try to bring your aunt into this. Someone must have hurt you to drive you here. There's no other explanation for a beautiful young woman's hiding away in that sleepy village."

"You're wrong. I love Banbury."

"Never married?" He looked skeptical. "Engaged?"

"Engaged once, but it wasn't a big tragedy when it didn't work. Our life-styles just didn't mesh."

"Let me guess. A traveling man?"

"Career Air Force, but that's not why I live in Vermont," she protested, annoyed by the knowing look on his face.

"Tell me about your family. What's your father's rank?"

"Why is that important?"

53

She'd chafed too often under a system where her father's rank in some obscure way determined her status among her peers who lived in base housing.

"It isn't, but you seem to resent the question. You must dislike the military caste system."

"I didn't like having my future decided by some faceless general in Washington."

"But your father must have reached a pretty high rank himself, judging by his daughter's abilities. Doesn't he have quite a bit of power himself over men in his command? Doesn't that reflect well on his family?"

"You're playing games with me," she said angrily. "Well, my father's a colonel, and I'm hardly ashamed of it; but it doesn't reflect on me one way or another."

"Of course it doesn't, Sara. Tell me, if you could have stayed in one place to grow up, where would you choose?"

"That's easy." She relaxed a little. "Sault Ste. Marie. My father was stationed at Kincheloe Air Force Base."

"In northern Michigan. They've closed that base now, haven't they?"

"Yes, some years ago, but our family had fun there. We lived in town for a change instead of on base. My brother played in a hockey league and could really fly on skates. I took figure skating lessons, and the whole family went snowmobiling. Naturally the next place we moved, they didn't even know what snow was."

"Vermont winters aren't likely to bother you then?"

"Hardly! I like hot summers and cold, snowy winters, not this dismal in-between weather. Where did you grow up?"

"Pennsylvania mostly. Southwestern part of the state. My father was a builder. He loved to take a rocky hill and plant a house on it, making it look like the darn thing just grew there. I don't think he ever put up a structure without a deck overlooking something."

"That's certainly different from what you do."

"Only partly. He taught me to take care with every

detail. Dad looked for the perfect site to build a new house. I look for perfect examples of old homes and try to restore them to what they once were. I hate tiled floors, walls paneled with sheets of pressed sawdust, and home handymen who don't know what they're doing. I once worked on a house where a former owner had pasted cheap tiles on all the floors, beautiful hardwood floors that needed only a little sanding and varnishing to be spectacular. Righting that mess was something I don't want to tackle again."

"You don't do all the work yourself?"

"Good Lord, no. I must have had thirty skilled tradesmen working at different times on the Attwater house, and that's not a big job. I do some tougher refinishing myself, though. Plaster restoration is tricky; I don't really trust anyone else to rebuild ornate details. I make a mold, of course, but it's touchy work."

He stopped abruptly, looking at her with mock anger. "You've done it again."

"Done what?"

"Led me down ego lane. Every time I ask about you, you end up listening to me spout off about my work."

"I enjoy hearing about it. Since I've gotten to know Aunt Rachel, I've become a fanatic about antiques."

"Forget Aunt Rachel. Forget antiques. Why are you really living here alone, looking for spinning wheels and going to high school band concerts? Next you'll tell me you have a cat."

"I don't."

"Good, I'm allergic to the beasties."

"I've always wanted one, however."

"It will take more than a hunk of fur to keep me away from your doorstep."

"This month maybe. What about after you start your job in Ohio? You won't be commuting back here for a Saturday night date."

"We met six days ago, we've barely begun our first

worthwhile conversation, and you're telling me what I won't be doing?" His tone was light, but his eyes had darkened angrily.

"May we leave now?"

"No, I want an after-dinner drink. What would you like?"

"Dessert," she said, fighting an impulse to sit pouting while he had his drink. "Cheesecake."

He attracted the attention of the waitress and ordered Scotch and water along with her dessert. Knowing she was being completely unreasonable, Sara still resented his easy charm with the young waitress. If he was trying to demonstrate what a nice guy he was with everyone but her, he was wasting his time.

"We were doing pretty well for a little while," he said, smiling across the cleared table as they waited for their waitress to return.

"I don't know what you mean."

"Now who's playing games?"

"Certainly not me. Would you excuse me for a minute please?"

He stood when she left to go to the rest room, following her with his eyes as she walked from the room. Powdering her nose wasn't going to buy her much time, but she couldn't think straight, looking across the table at Jason. Her better judgment told her this should be the last time she saw him, but her heart was sending out a conflicting message. She wished he had a huge wart on his nose, ears like sails, and a soprano voice, anything to break the hold he had on her senses!

Through the doorway to the commons room she could see him staring at the glass he was twirling idly with one finger and his thumb. Absorbed in his thoughts, he didn't see her until she reached their table.

"Don't stand," she said, quickly slipping into her chair.

"Your dessert," he said, gesturing.

"Looks delicious," she lied, gamely forcing herself to

nibble at small bites even though she was far too full and too agitated to want any.

"You don't want that any more than I want this drink. Don't eat it," he said, not trying to conceal his moodiness. "I paid the bill. Let's go."

He held her coat, then quickly slipped into the topcoat he wore over his tweed jacket and brown wool flannel pants. He ushered her outside before she had a chance to question him about why he was in such a hurry to leave.

He didn't release her arm until she sank down into the seat of his EXP. The car seemed to wrap itself around its occupants, encasing them in a comfortable metal capsule that shut out the rest of the world. Jason drove fast, but not dangerously so, making no attempt at conversation all the way to the front of her house. It wasn't a pleasant silence for Sara, but she was too cowardly to break it.

After releasing her safety strap, she moved to open the door herself, but his hand shot out to stop her.

"I'll get the door," he said curtly.

It wasn't worth fighting about, so she waited until he left the car and crossed in front to the passenger side. The hand he offered her was helpful; it was an upward stretch to extract all of her legs from the sporty car.

He kept his arm on her elbow as they walked to the front door, the bright green paint she'd applied invisible in the dark of night. Should she stop him from coming in? Could she? These questions had plagued her all the way home, and she didn't have a ghost of an answer.

"Give me your key," he said.

"I can open the door myself," she insisted. "Thank you for the dinner, Jason."

"Is this where I'm supposed to give you a quick peck on the cheek and vanish into the night?" he asked sarcastically.

"We haven't exchanged one sentence all the way here. There isn't much point in coming in."

"We haven't exchanged one sentence because I am coming in."

"I don't have any say in it?"

"I suppose you do if you want to scream bloody murder and bring the whole neighborhood down on my head."

"That's not my style," she said.

"I didn't think it was." There was a hint of familiar amusement in his voice again, but it didn't exactly please her.

She flicked on the dim light in the entry alcove and walked into the darkness of her living room, loosening the belt of her coat as she did.

"That dinner was so filling," she said. "Would you like a drink or some coffee?"

"No, that isn't what I want at all."

"It's a good night for a fire," she said a little nervously, feeling ill at ease because Jason seemed to fill the room, standing behind her with his coat still buttoned.

"May I take your coat?" she asked.

"You don't need to play hostess with me, Sara," he said, his words making her strangely shivery.

His tone made her turn to face him. She was not surprised when he bent to kiss her. Gently he tasted her lips, then deeply savored her response, slowly building an intimacy between them that made her feel as if an avalanche were sweeping down on her. He caught her shoulders, his hands still wearing leather driving gloves, and wrapped her against him, coat and all, pressing his mouth against hers. At first his assault was so forceful it hurt, but he quickly disciplined his demands, more gently kneading her lips with his until their kiss became mutually exciting. The tight low ache in her body was urgent and alarming as Jason slipped his tongue beyond her teeth, making their contact much more than a kiss.

Impatiently he pulled off his gloves, threw them aside, and gently stroked the fine hair on either side of her temples. His fingers traveled down the sides of her face and neck until they met the rougher texture of her coat. Then he spoke for the first time since kissing her. "Let me take your coat."

"It is warm," she said breathlessly.

He tossed first her coat and then his onto the closest chair. Resuming his kiss with patient persistence, his hands moving over the silky material of her blouse, exploring the contours of her shoulders and back with deceptive innocence, making her aware of every inch of flesh under his questing fingers.

Her lips felt bruised, but she didn't want him to stop kissing her when he did. Having moved only as far as the nearest table lamp, he turned it on low and tossed his jacket on top of their coats.

"Come here," he said, standing beside the couch.

His words broke her trance, and she stepped outside herself for a moment to absorb what was happening. His embrace hadn't been a good night kiss; Jason was going to make love to her. They'd been leading up to this moment all evening; everything else, even the disagreements that had surfaced so easily, had been a prelude. If she took a single step toward him, she'd plunge over the edge of a roaring torrent into the swirling depths of a whirlpool.

His arms were beckoning her, but she stood rooted to the spot, wanting to go to him more than she'd ever wanted anything, held back by a whole complicated maze of emotions. Making love with Jason wouldn't be a lark; it wouldn't be a casual act she could dismiss as unimportant. He wouldn't settle for that, she sensed, and she couldn't.

Her hesitation became so obvious that he couldn't will it away. He took the initiative, moving with slow steps that begged her to meet him halfway. Her one step barely nudged her from the spot, but it was enough. She was in his arms, kissing him urgently, trembling when his hand traveled down her spine to the rigid barrier of her belt. With fingers spread wide, he cupped her buttocks through the soft wool of her skirt, pressing her against him, nearly lifting her from the floor.

"Sara," he said, his voice sounding faraway.

Like a person watching a vision become reality, Sara saw all her premonitions about Jason coming true. He wanted her; that she could handle, but her own desire was racing out of control, driving away common sense, principles, and good intentions. The world had shrunk to this single confrontation between a man and a woman.

He pulled her beside him on the couch and buried his face in the hollow of her neck. She could feel the effort he was making to quiet his runaway passion, and when he looked up, his face was strangely softened.

Moving in slow motion, he lightly kissed her forehead, then barely touched his lips to each eyelid, his breath warm on her brow and strangely tranquilizing. Caressing the corner of each eye with slightly moistened lips, he made darts of pleasure shoot through her nervous system. A few fine wisps of hair clung to her ear when he pushed aside the heavy mass to explore her lobe with the tip of his tongue. With an audible shutter she sank back against the cushions, closing her eyes to mask the conflict raging in her head between what she wanted at this moment and what was best for the life she'd planned.

With a slowness that mesmerized her, Jason leaned over her and carefully slipped each button out of its hole until her blouse lay open but not parted. Her breasts ached to be caressed. Touching them lightly herself to ease the tension, she saw Jason smile knowingly.

How often had he worked his wiles on panting females? She tortured herself with an imaginary host of beautiful women, wishing that Jason were clutching and inexperienced, if only so she could be his first love. She tried not to think about Roger.

His hands found her bra clasp and released it easily, and she remembered that he was a man who did skilled work with his hands.

60

She sighed deeply when Jason trailed his fingers around the dusky rosiness of her breasts, kissing each so gently that a warm river of feeling flowed through her. He knew women's breasts were tender and sensitive; instinctively she knew he'd never prod and pummel them as though they were unfeeling lumps of dough.

Her involuntary moan told him all he needed to know. Her thighs became tight and hard when he slipped his hand between them, and he spoke in soft, coaxing tones. "I want you, Gilman, Sara."

She knew it, of course, but a wet drop escaped from one tear duct, her pleasure so intense it hurt. She was afraid of the emptiness that had to follow; nothing could feel so good for long.

"Can we go to your room?"

"My aunt Rachel," she said devilishly with one last attempt to turn aside what was happening.

"Your aunt Rachel is a myth. I don't believe in her. You've conjured her up out of a book of fairy tales, but she'll never come between us. Nothing will."

He stood and ran his hands under her knees, lifting her against him to carry her to her room. No man had ever tried to lift her without the buoyancy of a pool of water to help, at least not in the last twenty years, and she laughed in surprise.

"Put me down!" she cried out without wanting to be obeyed.

"You're not heavy."

"But I stick out all over."

Her skirt rode up way above her knees, and one long, slender leg threatened to slip from his grasp, dangling down toward the floor while the other toe pointed skyward. Her elbows didn't know where to go, and she felt about as graceful as a giraffe tipped over on its side.

"Put your arms around my neck, and stop kicking," he ordered without a trace of breathlessness or strain in his voice.

61

Cuddled more securely against him, she felt sure this could become her favorite means of transportation, but before she could say so, he'd located her bedroom. After switching on a light, he lowered her to the bed and leaned over her with eyes made liquid by desire.

"We're going to have fun, Sara."

Fun! It was the wrong word, and she stiffened, feeling the urgency of her body at war with deeper feelings. Limply she let him pull away her loosened upper garments, not resisting but not on fire as she had been under his onslaught of intimate kisses.

He loosened her belt and slid her skirt and half slip over her hips, first touching, then kissing the smooth skin above the pink triangle of her panties. After unbuttoning his shirt, he gathered her against him, crushing her breasts on the wiry softness of hair matted on his chest. Her toe brushed his shoe, and she squirmed, uncomfortable with her near nudity when he was still fully dressed.

"Can you tell me what I've done wrong?" he whispered.

She didn't know how to answer, but turning her face into the pillow wasn't enough to put off his question.

"Sara, you were with me," he said, trying to hide the hurt in his voice, "then suddenly you weren't. If I've hurt you, I need to know."

"No, you haven't hurt me."

Her voice was muffled, and she hoped she wouldn't be a baby and cry. She was telling the truth and lying, too. She did hurt, but no single act of his had caused it.

"Look at me."

He rolled her toward him in a no-nonsense way and held her face between hard hands. Minute pricks of darkness showed where his beard was beginning to surface, and an almost invisible white scar ran into his upper lip.

"How did you cut your lip?"

"My lip?" He instinctively ran a finger over his mouth. "Are you so interested in a scar I got in a bike accident twenty-five years ago?" He shook his head incredulously.

"I only wondered," she said weakly.

He rolled away from her and left the bed. He stormed to her closet to find her red quilted robe in the crush of clothes.

"Put this on," he said curtly. "I can't talk to you that way."

He went back to the living room, leaving her alone to put on her robe. Exhausted, racked by sensations she didn't want to deal with, she hoped that if she stalled long enough, he'd leave without seeing her again. It was a futile hope. He was staring into her fireplace grate with statue-like concentration when she finally ventured into the room.

"I rushed you, and for that I'm sorry," he said without looking at her. "But I still want to know, why the sudden turnoff?"

"I don't think I can explain."

"Don't think I'll leave until you do."

"I don't know myself," she said miserably.

"You're not"—he hesitated—"very experienced, are you?"

"You probably could say that," she said uncomfortably. "I haven't been married like you have."

"Oh, Sara."

He walked to her and gathered her in his arms, pressing her bowed head against his chest. His shirt was still open, and his hair tickled her nose. It was a new and pleasing sensation to cuddle against a man who towered six inches over her.

"It was when I said we'd have fun, wasn't it?"

She couldn't bring herself to answer.

"Maybe it was the wrong word, but I'm not just playing with you, Sara."

"You're leaving so soon it amounts to the same thing, doesn't it?"

"No! Sara, you can fly across this country in less time

than it takes to paint one room or mow a large lawn. Why are you so damn obsessed with places?"

"I'm not obsessed. I'm just not happy starting something that will end so quickly. I told you I hate losing my friends."

"I don't want to be your *friend!*"

He left her standing alone, putting on his jacket without bothering to button his shirt. He left that way, swinging his coat over his shoulder, banging the door behind him.

"Good-bye!" she called out to the closed door, pressing her knuckles against her temples to ward off the pain that threatened to engulf her.

She wasn't going to cry, she wasn't going to lie awake, and she certainly wasn't going to feel sorry for herself. It had to end this way. From the beginning she'd known that Jason wasn't for her; he was a nomad, a man who followed his interests wherever they took him, moving as frequently as he liked. His life-style was everything she'd rejected in Bill and more. Jason didn't even wait for the government to move him to the next assignment; he went on his own with all the zest of a traveling supersalesman.

Her arms were trembling; she had the most uncomfortable urge to make the veins on her inner elbow jump. Was she so upset that she was starting to twitch? No, she wouldn't give in to it. Jason Marsh was good-looking, aggressive, sexy even, but she hadn't known him long enough to let him really get to her.

Furious at herself for letting him come as close as he had, she crushed newspapers into balls and piled them around the birch log he'd earlier placed on her grate. In moments she had a column of flame racing up the chimney, and the well-cured log easily caught fire.

Tucking her feet under her on the couch, she watched the flames burn down to little tongues that lapped away at the solid log until it became a mass of glowing embers. Sometime before the cinders turned gray, Sara dropped into an uneasy doze.

Awaking cold and stiff in the early dawn, she was thankful for at least one thing: it was her Saturday off work. Weekend banking had infected Banbury, but at least it wasn't her turn to man a cage for the short three-hour morning stint. Bleary-eyed, she closed the flue over the dead embers in the fireplace and made a beeline for her bed, determined to sleep off the whole bad experience with Jason.

An hour later she gave up. Lying in bed remembering the warmth of his kisses and the persuasiveness of his touch was the worst therapy possible. She had laundry to do, a house to clean, and two weeks' worth of ironing. By noon Roger would probably call and ask her to a movie, an invitation she'd gladly accept. Her schedule didn't allow any time for regrets.

Her first call came from Aunt Rachel, who coyly wondered whether Sara had heard any more from "that wonderful Jason Marsh." "No" was the only possible answer. She could hardly explain to her great-aunt what had happened the night before; in fact, she couldn't even explain it to herself. Twice she'd gone with Jason against her better judgment, and last night she'd paid a high price.

Roger's call came just as she'd expected; in all fairness, she should have offered to fix dinner for him, but she didn't. She'd probably never hear from Jason again, but if she did, she didn't want Roger to be there when he called.

Not until she vacuumed in the afternoon did she find her missing shoe wedged under the edge of the couch. Holding it in her hand for a long moment before returning it to her closet, she wondered about the person she was becoming. Was she on her way to becoming a caricature of a spinster, so eager for male attentions that she'd jump at any chance?

Roger was in unusually high spirits.

"How about canceling the movie and going to a barn dance?" he asked, calling her back late in the afternoon.

"Fine," Sara agreed. "Where is it?"

"In the Moose Hall at Stafford. I'll pick you up around six thirty."

Riding through Stafford in Roger's gray Buick, Sara looked rather apprehensively on both sides of the street, but the distinctive shape of the EXP wasn't visible on Main Street. The town was a little larger than Banbury, or so it seemed because the Moose Hall and lumberyard extended the main drag an extra block.

Sara enjoyed square dancing, and Roger was unusually relaxed, going so far as to wear jeans and a yellow plaid shirt. Afterward they had hamburgers and malts at a local ice cream shop and drove back to Banbury at a leisurely speed.

In front of her house Roger slid across the car seat to be near her, kissing her warmly on her lips without his usual warm-up pecks.

"Tonight was fun," he said.

"Yes, it was. Thanks for taking me, Roger."

"It's always a pleasure to take you anywhere, Sara."

He kissed her again, pushing his tongue against her teeth. His lips were wet, and the air in the car had cooled quickly once the motor was off. Unfortunately his kiss was more clammy than exciting.

"I guess I'd better go in," she said, feeling a little guilty because she just wasn't in the mood.

"In a minute," he whispered.

He found an opening between two of her coat buttons and slid his hand against the front of her blouse.

"We've known each other for a while now," he said, obviously choosing his words with care. "I've hoped we could become . . . closer."

"We are good friends, Roger."

She kissed him quickly, missing most of his mouth, and opened the door for a quick retreat.

Alone in her house, she didn't feel proud of herself for making a hasty escape from Roger. On other dates she'd been perfectly willing to share small gestures of affection, but Roger rarely made them. Tonight she hadn't wanted him to touch her; Roger didn't make her feel the way Jason did, not at all.

Admitting this to herself was like acknowledging that she had a boil; it was extremely painful, and it made her feel flawed. Was she predestined to be hurt by the wrong men, never falling for one who could share the kind of life that was right for her?

Her yearning for Jason swelled, fed by her acceptance of the truth: She wanted him desperately.

The phone beside her bed sat in cold mechanical judgment, daring her to use it to ease the gnawing emptiness in her heart. If she could reach Jason by phone, would he offer to come to her then? Or would he be scornful, perhaps accusing her of teasing or leading him on? She'd never know, because the one thing she could never bring herself to do was approach this man.

## CHAPTER FOUR

The Banbury Bank did business in a white granite-faced building that dominated the main four corners of town. A small barbershop nestled against the lowest of its three stories on Locust Street, and the drugstore wall was flush against the Main Street façade. The bank had been built in the heyday of Art Deco architecture, and its original elegance was aging gracefully; the terrazzo floors, five latticework cages, and high arched ceiling still created the atmosphere of refinement their designers had intended. The board of directors had resisted modernization in any form, so the building stood as a monument to the town's last progressive era.

As a county institution the bank remained financially sound and reasonably busy, but Sara had never seen more than three cages open at once. On the rare occasions when summer people and farmers flocked in at the same time, Roger had to leave his more aloof position at a desk behind the railing and man a teller's slot. It didn't happen often.

Monday it was a relief to get back to work. She rode the elevator, a box of metal grillwork that allowed her to see the lawyers' offices on the second floor as she passed, up to the third floor, where an employees' lounge was across from an abstract company. The building's tenants existed cozily on their separate levels; a person could apply for a mortgage loan on the first floor and consult a lawyer about the deed on the second, while the attorney in turn could scurry up one more flight to have the deed validated. Vermonters didn't believe in senseless running around.

Sara preferred the steps to the elevator; climbing them was, in fact, faster, but because of some administrative peculiarity, it wasn't possible to use them to ascend. The doors on the first and second floors were locked from the outside; it was possible to descend, however, since the fire code was specific about not obstructing stairwell exits. Hurrying down the poorly lit, narrow steps, she was glad the weekend was over. She couldn't take another day at home, going over and over in her mind what had happened with Jason.

The day dragged, and when she had time to daydream, she forced herself to think of her plans for getting back into her own line of work. Her dream occupation was to run a country inn with a few rooms for guests and a dining room with luscious meals. She despaired of ever getting enough capital to own such a place, but much of her spare time was spent looking for possible openings as a manager or assistant manager in a food service position near Banbury. It was a quest that hadn't brought any results so far, not because she wasn't eligible but because few opportunities existed in her chosen area.

Sara much preferred serving the bank's patrons during business hours to the tedium of closing the books after the shades had been drawn for the day. Her late-afternoon work always seemed monotonous. Now that she had learned all she needed to know to do her job, the workday seemed to drag even more. Sundown came so early now that even though she had no qualms about walking Banbury's dark side streets, it was depressing to come out of the bank and find it was night.

"Sara!" A man caught up with her and touched her arm to bring her to an abrupt halt.

"Jason!" His name caught in her throat and came out barely audible, but surprise wasn't the reason. She never left a building or looked at a street without half hoping to see his EXP, even though her common sense told her she was being silly.

"How are you, Sara?"

"Oh, fine."

Fine was a piddling little word. Seeing him, she felt totally alive, her response unreasonably joyful. Every time she came upon him suddenly, it was like viewing him with a fresh pair of eyes; some feature or characteristic stood out and touched her in a new way. Today the wind gave his cheeks high color, making his face look leaner, and a slight crease in his forehead invited her to trace it with her finger, an impulse quickly repressed.

"Do you have your car?" he asked, his eyes riveted on hers, challenging her to try to evade him.

"No, I walked today."

"I'll give you a ride home. My car's just around the corner."

A gust of wind wrapped a strand of hair around her cheek, and she pushed it into place absentmindedly, weighing his offer uneasily. Coming from Jason, even the simple offer of a ride home seemed booby-trapped with complications. Before she could answer, the door of the barbershop opened, and Roger came out. He spotted Sara immediately and walked over to her.

"Sara, I thought I'd be done here before you left, but Ben's other barber was sick today."

Since she hadn't expected to see Roger or Jason that evening, she wished they'd both just say good-bye and let her go home alone.

"Oh, so you're Roger," Jason said, extending his hand with perfect Rotary Club heartiness. "Jason Marsh. Sara has told me a lot about you. President of the bank, right?"

70

"Well, only vice-president actually," Roger said, shaking hands and not minding his fictional promotion at all.

"We'll have to have lunch sometime," Jason said enthusiastically. "I've been working on the Attwater house in Stafford. The whole clan will be moving into the county after the first of the year. They should make fine residents, real assets."

Sara silently fumed, suspecting that Jason was deliberately baiting Roger with his Attwater connection. There was nothing like mentioning the word "asset" to attract a banker's attention.

She was about to walk away from the farcical conversation when Jason said, "Sorry I can't ask you to join Sara and me for dinner tonight. I'm stuck on a couple of details in the kitchen I'm renovating, and she's my resource person. We have to run over to Stafford for a while."

Roger's enthusiasm noticeably waned on hearing that Sara was tied up for the evening, but he seemed to find Jason's story perfectly feasible.

"Yes, Sara knows a lot about kitchens," he said. "Food management and all that. Well, see you another time, Marsh."

As soon as Roger was out of hearing, Sara turned on Jason. "We have no such plans!"

"I thought the one thing you liked about me was my work. This is a private home I'm restoring. You'd better take advantage of my offer and look at it while you can."

"Jason, I enjoy old places, but I'm not a fanatic. I don't drop everything just to wander around in the past. Antiques aren't my whole life."

"I've been trying to tell you they're not mine either, but why not take a look at the house? Satisfy your curiosity. I'd really like to show it to you."

"I don't know . . ."

"Sara, just once let's do something without debating it first."

She looked undecidedly in the direction of home, but

71

the pulling power of a hamburger patty and a salad wasn't that great. If she didn't go with Jason, she'd spend the evening thinking about him. Maybe the way to fight the hold he had on her feelings was to get an overdose of his high-handed, piratical ways. Judging by the act he'd staged with Roger, she should get tired of him pretty soon. Underneath their handshaking and geniality, the two men had been sizing each other up like wrestlers about to go to the mat.

"Oh, okay, I'll go," she said, sounding grudging even though she was curious to see the house.

"Sometime I'd like to hear you say, 'Thank you, I'd love to,' " he said.

"Why don't you try calling ahead of time and doing things the ordinary way?"

"Ordinary tactics don't work with you."

"I'll take that as a compliment."

He laughed.

"How did you happen to get the job with the Attwaters?" she asked when they were in the car and on their way.

"Through a mutual acquaintance."

"Is it a large house?"

"Wait until you see it. You can decide for yourself. Did you have a nice weekend?"

"Fine."

With Jason adroitly sidestepping her questions about the house, and Sara ignoring his guarded queries about how she'd spent the weekend, the ride to Stafford seemed to take a lot longer than the usual half hour.

The house recently purchased by the Attwaters was actually located on farm property on the outskirts of the small town. The approach road was narrow and unpaved, giving a feeling of isolation to the setting.

"I'm sorry it's too dark to see much outside," Jason said as he parked in a drive that swung past the side of the house and around the back. "This is one of the latest

72

examples of continuous architecture in the state. The barn and outbuildings were connected to the house. After 1800 not many houses were built this way."

"I don't think I'd like a bedroom down the hall from the pigs and cows, but maybe I'd feel differently if I had to shovel six feet of snow to get to the barn by daybreak."

"Unfortunately it wasn't a very sanitary convenience. Around 1870 a farmer with a huge family converted the old stable area and sheds to bedrooms and built a new barn away from the house. What we have here now is all residence."

Jason led the way over crushed gravel to the front, opened the door with a key, and let her proceed him into a large entryway.

"There are more refinements here than you'd expect in a farmhouse. It was built by a retired sea captain who made a bundle in the China trade. I guess he raised horses and played at being a gentleman farmer for a few years, but after his death the land was taken over by a working farmer."

"Wouldn't it be nice to retire young enough really to enjoy it?" she asked wistfully. "I love horses. I took lessons once, but not enough to be a good rider."

"My uncle had some horses on his property. We got to ride them in exchange for cleaning the stables, but at the time I was more interested in motorcycles."

"You can have those noisy things. I'll take a horse any day."

"Someday we'll go riding."

"Oh, no, I'd have to practice first. You'd laugh at me."

"Would that be so bad?"

It wouldn't, but she didn't say so.

Placing his hand lightly on her shoulder, he guided her into a room to the left.

"One thing you don't often find in farmhouses are carved wood fireplaces. The sea captain was pretty smart in planning his house. One good move was to locate the fireplaces on the outside walls instead of in the center of the house, which many builders were still doing them."

"We had a fireplace in the Soo, but I don't understand why the location should matter," she said, following him into a parlor, stepping around a ladder and a canvas tarp covered with paint cans.

"Much more comfortable. The warmth comes from the colder outer walls, where it's needed the most, and it doesn't get roasting hot in the middle of the house. It practically eliminated the problem of being wretchedly hot near the fire and freezing away from it."

"Did your father put fireplaces in the houses he built?"

"Usually, although he was on an iron stove kick the last time I saw him. Big custom-made monsters that are supposed to heat the whole house in winter."

"Do you see your parents often?"

"I try to drop in once a year at least. Sometimes I get pretty tied up."

He still had his hand on her shoulder, standing so close that their hips and legs touched, distracting her from the loveliness of the room.

"The gaslight fixtures weren't in the original house, of course," Jason said, pointing out delicate etched glass shades on the wall of the dining room, "but Mrs. Attwater was determined to keep them. They're electrified now, but I'd like to see you by gaslight."

"They're beautiful," she said, moving away from his arm to look more closely at them.

"They're nice, but I prefer to restore a room to the appearance it had when it was first built. Museum boards are usually more agreeable to that than private owners."

"I can understand why. They don't have to live like pioneers if that's what the house calls for."

"I make exceptions of conveniences like electricity, plumbing, and heating," he said affably.

He guided her from room to room, going upstairs first.

74

Even without furniture, the charm of the rooms was evident, and she loved the numerous fireplaces.

"Wouldn't it be wonderful to have a fireplace in the bedroom?" she said enthusiastically.

"I'd like to lie in bed and watch a roaring fire make shadows on the wall," he said, smiling at her, letting the words "with you" remain unsaid.

Unbidden, her mind conjured up an image of Jason naked in bed beside her, both of them warmed by an open blaze, but angry at herself, she quickly blocked the scene from her consciousness.

Leaving the kitchen till last, he showed her that room with special pride. Its fireplace had a huge open hearth, and even without the furnishings, Sara could imagine the women of the household spinning and doing needlework by firelight.

"The spinning wheel will sit here, won't it?" she asked wistfully.

"That's what the plan calls for."

"Will Mrs. Attwater ever use it, do you suppose? It's such a sturdy piece, in such good condition. I didn't want it as an ornament. Aunt Rachel is going to teach me how to spin."

"Mrs. Attwater will never use it." His voice sounded guarded.

With an irrational flash of jealousy, Sara imagined his client as a glamorous young jet-setter, interested only in having the house as a showplace to enhance her prestige.

"I didn't think so," she said, hard put to keep her voice neutral.

He came up behind her and touched her cheeks, making her skin tingle under his feathery caress.

"Mrs. Attwater has fingers like Polish sausages and such acute arthritis in her hands that she just manages to sign checks."

"Oh, how sad," she said, knowing she deserved to feel guilty, as she did. "She's not a young woman then?"

"Hardly. She wants this place as a vacation home for her grandchildren. Would it bother you if she were young?"

"Of course not," she protested rather too vehemently. "Why should your client mean anything to me?"

He turned her around and looked into her face with a knowing smirk.

"You could be just a tiny bit jealous of all the time I spend with her. I think I'd like that," he said just before his lips descended on hers.

His kiss was only a quick little nip, and he teased her by brushing the tip of her nose with his lips before taking her by the hand to finish the house tour.

"You love what you do, don't you?" she asked, her hand comfortably locked in his.

"Yes, I do. Too much maybe. If I see a beautiful house that's been abused or altered, I have a compulsion to see if I can chip and scrub and clean away all the damage. Guess I see myself as a sort of doctor for sick houses."

"I like that picture of you. I don't know how it looked before, Jason, but this house is lovely now. I'm really glad you showed it to me."

"My pleasure. Someday I'll show you the photos I took before we started. For example, the dining room had lime green wallpaper with big pink roses. Interesting what some people consider an improvement. My wife could never understand—"

He broke off so abruptly Sara knew he regretted mentioning his past. It was disconcerting that he'd said "wife," not "ex-wife."

"She didn't like your work?"

"Oh, hell, I suppose what she really didn't like was the way I live. She wanted a ranch-style existence in suburbia and a husband dancing attendance at her tennis club, bridge club, golf club, save-the-ducks club, whatever group was her latest mania."

"Oh," Sara said, sensing a condemnation of her own interests in his outburst.

"Don't look sorry for me," he said, scowling, misreading the look of pain on her face.

"I'm not, not at all. Most women want something like that, I guess."

"Anyway, she's married to a stockbroker in Philadelphia, and I can hardly remember what she looks like."

He thrust both hands into the pockets of his coat, walking toward the front entrance.

"This house is so inviting," she said, trying to cover the awkward moment.

"Thanks," he said dryly, switching off the lights.

Sara knew he regretted even mentioning his ex-wife. It depressed her to realize that the woman he'd married had found his nomadic life a trial, but Jason certainly hadn't changed the direction of his career because of it. Sara had to accept that he'd never give up his work for any woman; he was even less likely to do so now that he was a recognized expert in his field, undoubtedly very well paid as well as highly respected, although she sensed that the money and prestige were of secondary importance. Jason loved the old houses he restored, seeing his work as a mission to preserve the best of the past.

At the threshold she imagined that moving vans were coming at her from all sides, a mighty convoy trying to pound her into the ground. Throwing off the fanciful image with a shudder, she followed Jason out of the house.

"Hungry?" he asked as he locked the door behind them.

"I guess so."

"Well, don't commit yourself too firmly on that."

"Sarcasm as an appetizer?"

They never seemed to talk much riding in his car. Was it because he liked to concentrate fully on his driving or because they communicated better looking at each other face-to-face?

"Home," he said stopping in the driveway of a gloomy

77

late Victorian house with gray shingle siding near the main street of Stafford."

"Why are we here?"

"I have chili in the crock pot, the specialty of the house."

He led the way to a rear exit and up two flights of steps with brown rubber mats tacked on them. When the house was new, this might have been the servants' entrance.

"The third floor is all mine," he said, locating his key when they reached the upper landing.

His apartment was really one huge room spanning the attic level of the house, the side walls formed by the slant of the roof and recently covered with the same type of pressed board paneling Jason hated to find in houses he was going to restore. The area near the door was a kitchenette with a chrome-legged table and one spindle-backed wooden chair. The double bed was centered against one wall and covered with a vivid red and yellow spread in a geometric pattern and mounds of pillows in matching colors. A small television set was in the far corner with one green upholstered chair and a footstool. A dresser and some kitchen cupboards completed the furnishings.

"It certainly isn't what I expected," she blurted out.

"How did you think I live?" he asked. "Surrounded by highboys and parlor sets and gateleg tables?"

"I just thought you'd live differently. Are we picnicking on the floor, or do you have another chair hidden somewhere?"

"I'll use the footstool."

He smiled, lifted the lid of his crock pot to sniff appreciatively, and turned back to her to brush her forehead slightly with his lips.

"I can't believe you're the man who complained about wallpaper roses a little while ago," she said, giggling, as she walked over to finger the back of his upholstered chair, faded to a bilious pea soup shade.

Laughing off her comments, he said, "I hadn't noticed

78

before. That chair is an atrocious color, isn't it? You can tell I live with my work; all I do here is sleep."

"You're not your own decorator then?"

"The bedspread and pillows were my only contribution to the decor. I thought the place needed a bright touch with all that fake walnut paneling, but I'm pretty tired of them. I'll leave them for the landlord when I go."

"You really do travel light."

"I've been too busy gaining experience, expertise, to collect things. Maybe someday—"

"Where should I put my coat?"

"Oh, sorry. That wall to your left has a handle. The closet door is made of paneling, too."

The concealed storage area ran the length of the house, she noticed when she hung her coat on a rack inside it, and several boxes of books on the floor showed that Jason wasn't entirely without possessions. Still, she watched him put their meal on the table with puzzlement, wondering what new facet of his character he'd reveal next. He'd been right about one thing the first time they spoke on the road by the auction barn. Curiosity was the right bait to use with her, and hers was constantly being piqued by this contradictory man. He'd dedicated his life to restoring gracious, lovely houses but seemed content to live in a drab room with only one window at the end partly blocked by an air conditioner, overlooking a parking lot.

After pushing the stool up to the table with his foot, he seated her on the chair, painted black but showing layers of yellow and white in chipped patches. After setting the crock pot on the table, cord dangling over the edge, he dished out liberal portions with a tablespoon, filling two Styrofoam bowls to the brims.

"Your bowls are lovely."

"Well, they save dishwashing," he said, grinning and pushing a paper plate of warm hard rolls toward her.

Taking one and breaking it in half, she arched her

brows, indicating the shower of crusty little crumbs scattered on the table.

"Sorry, that's my last paper plate. Use your napkin," he said, buttering his roll with exaggerated nonchalance.

"Shall I pour?" she asked, nodding toward the coffeepot sitting on the stove.

"Be my guest. The mugs are in the cupboard to the right."

She found two chipped ironstone mugs and not much else in the cupboard, then filled them with strong black coffee perked in the old-fashioned way on a stove burner.

"How often do you eat at home?" she asked.

"Cooking that bad?"

"No, the chili is very good, but I've never seen tableware quite like yours." She waved a heavy old silver-plated knife with a rounded end that looked as if it'd been caught in a garbage disposal.

"Oh, I leave stuff like that behind. When I get to a new place, I just stop at the first garage sale I see and restock. I eat only one meal out of fifty at home anyway."

"This is a crash pad, not a home."

"Home is where the heart is."

"I've heard that somewhere," she said, smiling. "Guess I'm honored to hit one of your at-homes."

"Doubly honored. I made the chili just for you."

"Jason, you're impossible! You couldn't know I was free tonight."

"No, but chili keeps."

After rinsing their cups and utensils under hot water, he set the whole crock pot with the remaining chili in it into the refrigerator.

"Now we'll go meet your aunt Rachel."

"My aunt Rachel?" she gasped.

"Aunt Rachel is a real person, isn't she?"

"Of course, but—"

"We could watch television, but my set gets only black

80

and white fuzz. You can guess the only other way to entertain ourselves here."

Following his glance toward his bed, she flushed. The man had a genius for catching her off-balance!

"You're playing your space game again," she accused him when she turned around quickly and nearly collided with him.

"No, I'm not playing."

He kissed her at the top of her nose right between her wide-open eyes, making her feel strangely disoriented. Teasingly his lips slid down her nose, lightly kissing the tip.

"If I really kiss you," he growled, "I won't get to meet the only member of my fan club tonight. Should we call her first?"

"I can't believe you're actually willing to call before you drop in."

"I'm gallant with older women. That's why they adore me."

Every window in Aunt Rachel's roomy two-story house showed a light, and Sara almost expected to see Christmas lights strung from the swinging wooden gate to the rails of the front porch to illuminate the path for the celebrity guest.

"Mr. Marsh, it's such an honor to meet you," her great-aunt said, opening the door before they had a chance to turn the knob of the old-fashioned handbell.

Five minutes later she wondered why she bothered to stay with the two of them. Her diminutive white-haired relative was flirting outrageously with Jason, plying him with more hastily defrosted goodies from her oversize freezer than any human should consume in a month. Rachel looked a little disappointed when he declined a third date-nut bar to go with his coconut-lemon cookie.

Sara smiled indulgently at her aunt, glad that there wasn't any younger competition in town with Rachel's charm and vitality. A single girl didn't stand a chance with her around. It was a family tragedy that Rachel's fiancé had been killed fighting in the South Pacific in 1944, and no man had ever appeared to take his place. This was no reflection on Rachel's ability to be an absolute angel with any man who even mildly pleased her, and Jason seemed to please her a great deal.

"I'm completely entranced," Jason said several hours later when they were getting into his car after saying good night to Aunt Rachel. "That woman is a real wonder."

"Isn't she special? Having her so close, I hardly remember to miss the rest of my family."

"Home now?" he asked.

"Yes, please."

On her porch he took the key from her hand, pushed the door inward, and let her enter first.

"Thank you for showing me the Attwater house," she said. "And for the dinner."

"Thank-you's are what people say when they're parting for the night," he said, taking her in his arms in the dark entryway.

"Jason . . ."

His kiss barely brushed the corner of her mouth, but it ignited a whole battery of sensations.

Shedding his coat as he walked, he moved with easy familiarity to the nearest lamp. The black pullover he wore emphasized the gleaming darkness of his eyes, and again she imagined that he was Blackbeard on the deck of his frigate, holding life-and-death power over a terrified captive. To break the spell, she quickly removed her coat and stamped imaginary snow from her feet.

"It's really feeling like winter," she said with false bravado, rubbing her hands together vigorously even though she'd only had a short ride in a warm car.

He watched her with the same look that had appraised auction goers who might have tried to outbid him, a bold stare that stripped her of all defenses.

"I want you," he said bluntly, then more softly, "I need you."

She turned away, holding her coat like a shield. When he came to her and touched the base of her neck, she shuddered, letting her coat drop to the floor.

With gentle strokes he kneaded her shoulders, then slid the jacket of her tailored gray-flecked jacket down her arms. Behind her now, he enveloped her in his arms until she rested against the hard length of his body. She could feel his heart beat and hear the sharp intake of breath into his lungs when his hands cupped the swell of her breasts.

"We need to talk," he said in a muffled voice, his hands sliding down her torso, exploring the contours of her body with unhurried enjoyment.

"Yes." She could hear the unsteadiness in her voice as tension tightened her muscles, making her lean away from him, her spine rigid, her buttocks contracted, resisting him.

"Come sit by me," he said, feeling the loss of her soft pliancy.

Sitting by him on the couch, she felt like a drowning woman, clutching at her last wisps of resolve to prevent total catastrophe.

"You look terrified," he said grimly.

"No, not that."

"Don't be afraid of me."

He leaned forward to kiss her tenderly on both cheeks, then pushed aside her hair to fill her ear with the exploring tip of his tongue. Raw yearning made her body quiver, and he pulled her onto his lap, sliding his hand between her skirt and blouse. Rubbing her back gently, he sighed with contentment when she finally relaxed against him, her fingers slipping into the thick hair at the back of his head. Resting his lips against hers, he slowly unclasped her bra, reaching under the loose cloth. Groaning deeply, he locked his mouth on hers, kissing her with fervor.

"I know you like this," he whispered into her hair,

running two hard fingers over the mound of her breast. "Don't go cold on me again."

"I don't know if I can help it," she said miserably.

"A lot of things seem to be happening that neither of us can help," he said softly. "It's come over me so suddenly, this feeling I have for you, Sara. I keep expecting to wake up and find it's only a dream."

"We really don't know each other," she said almost to herself.

"No, but you've become terribly important to me. Sara, I didn't plan it. I didn't want to care for anyone as much as I do for you, but it's happened."

"I can't believe—"

"You will. Sara, this isn't something I want just for tonight. I've admitted that to myself already, and my senses are still reeling from the impact. I think you feel something for me, too."

"Yes, but I'm not ready."

"Not ready for me to make love to you? Or not ready for any change in your life?" he asked, pushing her for an answer while his hand moved rhythmically over her waist, moving under her skirtband to be stopped by resisting hands.

"I don't know!" she cried out, distracted by the shock waves of desire assaulting her.

"Don't look away," he ordered. "You do that too often. Just when I think I've gotten past that guarded look of yours, you pull up the drawbridge again."

"Do I do that?" she asked, stricken by his criticism.

With ringing ears and clouded senses, she pulled his head against hers, pouring all the force of her frustration into their raging, enveloping kiss.

Together they slid to the floor, his leg unnecessarily making her a prisoner. Holding and being held, she felt weak against the strength he was keeping in rein. When he was passive for a moment, she ran her hand over the swell of his shoulders and chest, studying his face until, with a low moan, he sat forward to peel off his shirt. His upper arm was hard under her cheek, and she buried her face against his side, closing her eyes to hide the pleasure she felt.

He took her hand in his and put it back on his chest, stroking it with his fingers.

"Touch me," he said. "Let your hand roam where you want it to."

"Oh, Jason, I can't. This just isn't right for me!"

"Don't you ever follow your instincts?" he asked angrily, sitting up and holding her face so she couldn't avoid his gaze. "Are you trying to tell me it's wrong for us to feel this way? Is it a bad thing to make love to a person you care about?"

"It's wrong to get involved! We'll hardly even have time really to get to know each other. You'll be hurt, I'll be hurt. There isn't anyplace in your life for me, and I can't be what you want."

"Not if all you want is a banker who will mow the lawn every Saturday and spend two weeks every August playing croquet in the Catskills."

The anger in his voice hurt more than his words, and she recoiled as if she'd been slapped. Unexpectedly he gathered her into his arms, kissing her urgently, punishing her mouth, entangling his fingers roughly in her hair.

"Tell me you want me to stay the night, Sara," he urged, speaking into the hollow of her neck.

It was what she wanted more than anything at this moment, but the words wouldn't come. If he would just let it happen, she knew she wouldn't resist, but how could she issue an invitation? If it hurt this much being with him, how could she stand the pain when he left for good?

"I can seduce you, I think," he said cruelly, running his hands under her skirt to the edge of elastic on her pantyhose. "Maybe you want me to arouse your body, so you won't share the responsibility for what happens. You can blame me instead of admitting to yourself that you want me as much as I want you."

His hands slid downward, massaging her so intimately that she felt heat rushing to her groin.

"You're trembling," he said, crushing her with the weight of his body, straining against her until she cried out in longing. Suddenly he released her and rose to his feet in one hasty motion.

"Jason!" His name escaped her throat, even though she wouldn't give voice to the plea in her heart.

She stood because she couldn't bear to have him towering over her, his face scornful and hard.

"It won't be that way," he said angrily. "I don't want you unless you're honest enough to admit you want me."

"I don't!" she lied. "I've never been a one-night stand for any man."

"That's not what this will be!"

"One night, one month, it amounts to the same thing. Why can't you just leave me alone?"

"Because I don't think that's what you really want."

He captured her in his arms, grinding her against him until the hard thrusts made her dizzy with longing.

"You see how it could be," he said tauntingly.

He released her so suddenly that she stumbled, grasping the edge of the couch to keep from falling. With fast, angry movements he pulled on his shirt and then his coat, turning to look at her with lips drawn into a thin, hard line and eyes blazing furiously.

"Think about me when you're lying awake in that cold little spinster nest of yours."

Enraged beyond endurance, she threw the first thing that her hand found. It was only a sofa pillow, but it hit him squarely in the face before dropping to the floor, bringing a flush of high color to his cheeks.

"Next time you throw something at me," he said angrily, "I'll turn you over my knee."

"There won't be a next time. Get out of my house!"

He smiled, but it didn't change the cold, hard expression in his eyes.

The door closed behind him, and Sara felt choked by her anger. With impotent rage she kicked at the fallen pillow, smarting under his threat. She could hear his car peel away from the curb, shattering the quietude of her neighborhood just as carelessly as he'd knocked apart all her composure and self-control.

What made her so furious, she thought, tears of despair forcing their way from her eyes, was that he was right. She wasn't strong enough to resist his seductive powers, but physical capitulation wasn't enough for him. He wanted her to admit she wanted him, to confess that he'd become so important to her that she couldn't deny him. The greedy pirate wouldn't settle for her body; he wanted her soul, too!

Maybe if she pleased him in bed, he'd pack her up along with his two chipped cups and his crock pot to haul her off to Ohio. Ohio! Then what? Connecticut? Alabama? Oregon? Did it really matter where a camp follower went?

Nights with Jason Marsh might be exciting, even wonderful, but what about the long, empty days? While he worked salvaging the best of the past, what would she be doing? Her life would be one long series of barren apartments and purposeless jobs. How long would it last? One year? Five years? Thirty?

She wasn't even sure Jason wanted to take her with him, she thought, sobbing blindly now as her head throbbed. When she couldn't cry anymore, she splashed gallons of cold water over her swollen eyelids and crawled into bed. She slept when weariness finally blotted out her remorse.

# CHAPTER FIVE

Awake long before her alarm clock rang, Sara wanted to return to the oblivion of sleep, but it eluded her. Even when she lay motionless, her mind was working like a film projector, flipping back and forth between forward and reverse, always coming back to Jason, replaying the scenes with him in a jumbled, unfocused way.

She was falling in love; she was in love, yet Jason was a threat, the personification of all she'd come to Banbury to avoid: impermanence, uncertainty, restlessness. He was aggressive, self-assured, overconfident, characteristics that were blurred by charm and magnetism when he chose to be attentive. Physically he appealed to her more than any man she'd ever met. Tall and well proportioned, he was powerful without being weighed down by heavy masses of muscle. His waist was slender with only the slightest wrinkle of flesh when he leaned forward without his shirt, and his hands fascinated her, the fingers blunt and square-nailed but capable of tasks that required the utmost delicacy. When he touched her, spasms of sheer pleasure shot through her body, lighting a fire that was still raging, unchecked.

Pressing her forehead into her pillow, she remembered

her impression of his apartment, a long, barren room that lacked even the appeal of a gypsy wagon. The emptiness of it, the temporary atmosphere screamed of his disdain for domestic life; his work was his be-all and end-all, the only thing that really mattered to him. What chance did a woman have with a man who was totally obsessed with his job, to the exclusion of even his personal comfort?

Preferring activity to lying in bed with her unsettling thoughts, she got up and padded barefoot on cold floorboards to the window looking out on her backyard. A thick ring of shrubs and trees made it a private haven ideal for sunbathing in the summer; but now the leaves were gone, and she could see the backyards of the houses facing the next street. The deep gray of early dawn made even freshly painted buildings look dingy, and she wished, not for the first time, that the family directly in back of her would haul away the rusty junk car sitting unused beside its garage.

No paradise on earth, she reminded herself glumly as she knelt to locate her slippers, which she'd accidentally kicked under the bed.

In the kitchen she brewed some herbal tea, then carried the beverage with its spicy apple fumes into the living room to see if she could catch a weather report on television.

Setting her tea beside the couch, she noticed the needlework pillow she'd thrown at Jason and stooped to gather it into her arms. Holding it in midair, ready to toss it back on the sofa where it belonged, she looked at it as if she'd never seen it before. A long-ago project of hers, it was a little dingy now from constant use, but the words worked in wool were still vivid in the original shades of brown and yellow and orange. She studied the intricate pattern, a stylized hearth scene, and read what was written there in yarn: "Home is where the heart is."

When Jason had used this familiar quotation, she'd actually forgotten that it was on her pillow. How strange that people sometimes stopped seeing things when they became a familiar part of their everyday background.

Hugging the old pillow to her cheek, she felt a hot, bitter tear trickle down her face. She loved Jason, loved him against all reason, loved him hopelessly, painfully, and overwhelmingly. Admitting it to herself made her only more dejected, more torn between what her heart was telling her and what she knew was right for her future.

Less than a year ago it had been Bill. Was she so ripe for love that she gave her heart away to any man who could stimulate her glands? It was a sobering thought, one she normally would have found humorous.

She tried to conjure up a mental picture of Bill as she sipped her tea, but Jason kept intruding, washing out the image of the young airman. Bill's courtship had been exciting, sometimes fun and sometimes nerve-racking. He wouldn't have left her last night without pressing his advantage; in fact, one of the many sources of tension between them was her reluctance to have him as her lover before their marriage. Their lovemaking had been steamy and demanding, coming close to but never quite reaching consummation. Sometimes she satisfied him in other ways; she never satisfied herself except with the conviction that there was plenty of time after they were married to be totally together.

With Jason it was commitment, not his ardent advances, she feared. She wanted him in a way she'd never before experienced. Out of the boiling confusion of her emotions, she gleaned the truth: Jason was the first man she'd ever loved completely, and he was the worst man she could have chosen.

In spite of her love for Jason, she just couldn't face living the rest of her life as an outsider, a stranger who said hello and good-bye in the same year. Too many new schools, too many hostile and indifferent faces had conditioned her from childhood to value the known friend, the familiar face.

Jason was robbing her of her peace of mind, disturbing the life she'd always yearned to build for herself. She was just starting to become part of a warm, friendly, stable community, and her love for him was threatening to cast her out again.

She didn't know how deep his interest ran, but nothing in his past made her believe that she meant more to him than a temporary diversion. This was a perfect time for him to have a brief affair with a local woman; his work was nearly done, and he could easily avoid any strings simply by leaving. Commitments were for legal contracts, he'd said, and obviously he was very wary of building any lasting relationships. In fact, he probably had more leisure time now than he had had since his arrival. Most of the work to be done required only casual supervision from him. Why not kill time dallying with her until he was free to leave?

Impatiently she carried her empty cup back to the kitchen, struggling to shrug off the self-pitying mood that was so alien to her nature. She wasn't the only woman to suffer because she was attracted to the wrong man. Jason would leave; the pain would subside. All she had to do was ride out the storm and let time heal the wound.

Red woolly wedge-shaped potholders resembling slices of watermelon hung over her stove, a housewarming gift from Aunt Rachel. They reminded her that once her great-aunt had cried over a young sailor dead in battle, but no one ever saw Rachel lose her zest for life. Sara could do the same, put aside an ill-advised love without letting it cripple her life.

Roger was reserved with her at the bank that morning, perhaps displeased that she'd gone off with Jason the previous evening. Sara countered by being unusually forward. Once she hadn't wanted to encourage Roger too much until she knew how serious their friendship might become. Now she knew exactly what her feelings were; she loved a man who was totally wrong for her, and the warm companionship of a good friend like Roger looked like a sensible antidote. Her conscience nudged her just a bit, making her wonder if she was using Roger unfairly, but she was sure nothing in their relationship had changed. She was only acknowledging the importance of their friendship. On the night of the barn dance Roger had certainly given her reason to believe he wanted them to become closer.

"It's been a long time since I fixed dinner for you," she said to him when business hit a midmorning slack period. "If you can put up with my steak and mushroom sauce another time, I can have it ready around seven."

"That sounds great to me," he said, smiling at the prospect of his favorite meal.

"Good. Don't bring wine. I have some."

She smiled with perverse satisfaction at the prospect of serving Jason's wine to Roger. The label was one she didn't recognize, and she wondered if it was a special favorite of the donor.

With no formal dining room, she set up her card table in the living room, using a white drawnwork linen cloth, one of her auction prizes, and her favorite tall intaglio-cut glass candlesticks, found at a bargain price at a house sale. The table was directly in front of the large bay window facing the street, but she didn't draw the drapes. If Jason made one of his unheralded appearances, he'd be able to see she was occupied for the evening. Angering him had nothing to do with making her dinner visible; she was running her defensive team, not the offense. If she had wanted to encourage Jason, she wouldn't try to make him jealous. The dinner would be for him.

As hastily planned as it had been, the evening went smoothly. Roger was a good conversationalist when he made the effort, and they shared many interests. As long as she could steer him away from his family's long but not particularly exciting history, their discussions were entertaining.

She'd pulled out all the stops to make a delicious but necessarily quick dinner for him. The frozen asparagus worked out fine with her secret instant hollandaise recipe, and a dessert with flaming cherries pleased Roger so much she didn't let him suspect how easy it was to prepare. If anything, their meal was too successful; both of them became sluggish and sleepy from eating too much, and Roger left early so he'd be sharp for a business meeting in the morning. He kissed her three times at the door, complimenting her for the dinner again.

She was just cleaning up the last of her cooking mess when there was a knock on the kitchen door. Most townspeople, her great-aunt included, favored the rear door, reserving the front for more ceremonial calls, but Sara certainly wasn't expecting a neighbor at this time of night. Early to bed was the rule on her street.

"Dinner party over?" Jason asked when she opened the door.

Her heart pounded in double time, but not because she was surprised; every time she opened her door she nourished a furtive hope that Jason would be on the other side. With hands thrust into the pockets of his sheepskin-lined coat, he leaned against the doorjamb, feigning indifference but looking like a jungle cat about to pounce on its prey. With an effort she composed her features, hoping he wouldn't suspect the effect he had on her.

"If you know I had company, you must know he's gone."

"Your front curtain is the only one you left open deliberately, so I couldn't see the whole house. Although I assume that boxcar Buick was your banker's."

"Did you come here to insult my friend's taste in cars?"

"Damned if I know why I'm here. Maybe this bug I've got is like influenza; the fever will burn it out eventually."

"Well, I've never been compared to a virus before."

"I'll bet you haven't. I'm driving up your heating bill, standing here with the door open."

He stepped forward, leaving her little option but to admit him unless she wanted to throw a body block at him. She didn't.

"I had a lousy dinner at the drugstore."

"I didn't know it served dinner."

"Ham on stale rye and a milk shake."

"You must be used to fast sandwiches on the run."

"Why do you say that?"

"The way you live . . ."

"I'm in your house thirty seconds, and we're back to that."

"I'm not back to anything, but I am tired. I had planned to go to bed early tonight."

"You look a little frazzled. Didn't you sleep well last night?"

"I slept fine!"

"I didn't. I haven't let a woman tease me the way you do since high school."

"Me tease you?"

He shrugged his shoulders, dismissing the subject.

"Well, anyway, you missed a chance to eat at Sibley's Tavern again. It closes for the season at the end of the month, you know."

"We were just there. Somehow I'll make it through the winter without going there again."

"Do you ever think of getting back into the restaurant business yourself?" he asked, watching her wipe off the stove burners, taking off his coat and draping it on the back of a kitchen chair.

"Maybe someday, if an opportunity turns up around here."

"It has to be here?"

"You know it does. I'm buying this house. I intend to stay here for good."

"I can't believe moving was that painful for you. Look

at the friends you made, the countries you saw. Can you imagine growing up in Banbury and never knowing any other place?"

"The people here are kind; the schools are good; it's not too far from larger cities. There are worse places to grow up."

"And better."

"That's debatable."

He wandered into the living room, and when she followed a minute later, he was standing over her cloth-covered card table, cleared except for the empty wine bottle.

"Did you enjoy my wine?"

"It was very good, thank you."

"I'll bet it was."

"You did give it to me."

"I didn't say I objected to your sharing it with your bank president."

"Vice-president," she corrected, burning because she knew he deliberately baited her by making Roger's job sound stuffy.

"Mind if I turn on your TV?"

"I'm surprised you're asking before you do it."

"There's a game I want to watch. My set is shot, I guess."

"You could get a new one, but then you'd have something to move, wouldn't you? Anyway, there's no football on tonight."

"There's a hockey game," he said, adjusting her portable color set to his satisfaction.

"Oh, hockey can be exciting."

"This is just an exhibition game, I think."

Having sat down in the middle of her couch, he stretched his sweater-clad arms over the tops of the cushions and stuck his legs out full length across her earth-toned carpet, seeming to fill the whole room.

"It never matters to me whether it's a league game or

not. I don't care much who wins. It's just fun to watch how well the players skate," she said.

"Watch it with me. Sit down."

He removed one arm from its resting place and invitingly patted the cushion beside him.

"No, I have to clean up."

"You look clean enough to me."

"The kitchen isn't. There're things I have to take care of," she alibied, hoping he wouldn't ask what.

"Suit yourself. Got a beer?"

"No, I hate beer."

"Roger hates it, too?"

"He's not crazy about it."

"Coffee?"

"Oh, all right, I'll make some, but I'm going to bed pretty soon. You'll have to leave then."

"I'll leave as soon as the game is over," he said absently, seemingly absorbed in the fast-moving action on the screen.

She made jobs for herself as long as she could, feeling so drawn to the living room that it took a supreme effort of will to keep from sitting beside Jason on her couch. After refilling his coffee cup a second time, she rinsed the pot, determined not to play hostess for a minute longer.

"What period is it?" she asked, glancing at the set he was staring at avidly.

"Nearly the end of the first. The Bruins are ahead one to nothing."

"I really would like to go to bed now, Jason."

"I'll turn out the lights and lock the door when the game is over. Have a good sleep."

"You can't just stay here," she said, flustered by his casual use of her home.

"Why not? I'll turn the sound down so it doesn't keep you awake."

"Oh, watch your hockey then," she said, giving up.

96

"Why don't you watch with me? You said you like the game."

"Not well enough to lose sleep watching it. I'm going to bed."

"Good night," he said, seemingly absorbed in the game. "Oh, before you go, do you have any popcorn?"

"No, no, I don't."

"Too bad. Cereal?"

"Just help yourself to whatever you can find. Good night!"

He was the one who turned down the volume and closed the hallway door, but it was his presence, not the sound of the television, that kept her turning restlessly in bed. When her bedside clock showed that it was after midnight, she pulled on her robe and crept down the hallway, opening the door a crack to see Jason stretched out sound asleep on the couch, a movie melodrama from the 1930s playing on the TV.

"Jason. Jason!" she said, hoping to wake him by calling his name, but not succeeding.

After nudging his shoulder gently, she stepped back as soon as he showed signs of waking.

"You fell asleep," she said, feeling it was unfair of him to keep her awake when he'd dozed off so easily.

"I guess I did." He sat and rubbed the sleep from his eyes. "Who won the game?"

"I have no idea. I went to bed."

Sitting and stretching his long, muscular legs, he made her think of a grizzly bear coming out of hibernation. His hair was tousled, and his eyes were dulled by sleep; but she had to resist an urge to cuddle him, reminding herself that bears are dangerous when they first wake up.

"What time is it?" he asked, yawning.

"Nearly twelve thirty."

"Oh, I've got to go. I have a furnace repairman coming at seven in the morning."

"Are you awake enough to drive?"

"Do you have a spare bed?"

"No, I use the other bedroom for a sewing room, but you could stay on the couch."

"If that's your best offer, I'll drive home. Your couch is too short."

With his coat on and car keys in hand, he turned back to her, still looking too sleepy to operate his car on the dark, narrow road to Stafford.

"How about tomorrow night?" he asked. "Can I pick you up around seven?"

"No." She shook her head for emphasis.

"You don't even know what I have in mind."

"It doesn't matter. I'm going to Roger's house for dinner."

"Roger's cooking?"

"No, his mother."

"He lives with his mother?"

"And his father."

"Cozy group," he said in a voice that made her want to throw something at him again. "Well, have a nice time."

He shut the door behind him but immediately opened it again, playing with the catch impatiently.

"This lock isn't catching the way it should. Better have a locksmith replace it," he said. "I don't think it's anything I can fix."

"I wouldn't ask you to!"

"Well, thanks for the use of your TV—and your couch. Good night."

Her lower lip was trembling when she locked the door after him and shut off the television and lights. She pressed her fingers against it, puzzled and upset by Jason's drastic change of tactics. He acted as if he really had come just to watch a hockey game, and he hadn't even tried to kiss her before he left.

Dinner the next evening with Roger's parents was everything she expected it to be: a seminar on family history.

Since neither his scholarly father nor his somewhat nervous, chatty mother added anything to the yarns Roger had already told her, she was grateful when they suggested playing bridge after dinner. She and Roger made a good partnership, taking advantage of his father's talkativeness to win two rubbers in a row. There was interest in starting a duplicate bridge club in town, and Roger was one of several skilled players learning how to direct it. Both he and Sara looked forward to earning master points in their own community when the group got organized.

Later that night, getting ready for bed, Sara realized again how well her interests corresponded with Roger's. Maybe, someday . . . but the disturbing image of Jason Marsh intruded on her thoughts, making sleep an elusive blessing again that night.

She rarely got personal calls at the bank; her great-aunt, the only one likely to call during business hours, worked at the school until nearly dinnertime, preferring to finish her work in her classroom instead of taking it home. Even first-grade teachers had desk work, she often explained to her friends. Sara had several women friends in the town, but they, too, worked during the day and were more likely to call her at home than at the bank. Since Roger was working at his desk, she was almost certain that a late-afternoon summons to the phone meant Jason was calling.

"Are you available tonight?" he asked brusquely, not bothering to say hello.

"I'm sorry, Jason, no."

"Roger?"

"Does it really matter what I'm doing?"

The phone went dead in her ear.

She and Roger never spent the whole weekend doing things together. He religiously checked not only on his brother's family but on his grandparents, aunts, uncles, cousins, and assorted distant relatives, duty calls Sara

99

admired him for making but had no wish to share. With a flash of inspiration she offered to drive Aunt Rachel into Brattleboro for some early Christmas shopping. Her aunt was delighted, agreeing immediately that it would be fun to make a weekend of it and spend Saturday night in a hotel.

Coming home from their shopping excursion on Sunday afternoon, Sara was easily convinced to look at a few old houses, each conveniently occupied by old friends of her great-aunt. By the time she dropped off Aunt Rachel and reached her own house it was well past six in the evening. If Jason had tried to call her, she was happier not knowing about it. She and Roger were playing bridge with the bank president, John Hadley, and his wife at seven o'clock, so it took a mad dash for her to change her clothes and be ready on time.

"What we need to remember"—Roger coached her on the way to the Hadleys' huge boxlike house on Saylorville Road—"is that his wife always leads away from kings. She loves to play no-trump, too, so it's easy to catch her short in at least one suit. We'll try to sit so I lead on the hands she plays. Watch my first card, and remember to lead it back every chance you get."

Sara agreed automatically with Roger's strategy, but when they were actually playing with their pleasant opponents, she enjoyed hearing about Marge Hadley's grandchildren more than she did playing cutthroat bridge. In spite of Roger's frowning, silent reminders, she forgot to return his lead several times and overbid her own hands attempting to recoup. It didn't matter to her that they lost two out of three rubbers by a narrow margin, but Roger was taxed playing the good sport for his employer.

Sara barely listened to him on the way home, but Roger was too preoccupied rehashing every losing hand they'd played to notice. After pulling into her drive, he kissed her three times rather absentmindedly, still too distracted by the bridge game to give her his full attention. Sara assured him she didn't need to be escorted to her door.

Roger drove away as soon as she reached the porch, leaving her to grope for her key in darkness since she'd forgotten to turn on the porch light before she left. Reaching for the storm door, she nearly stumbled over an obstacle sitting there. Picking it up and finding it heavy, she balanced it on one hip while she opened the inner door. Even without lights she knew what it was: a bag with two six-packs of beer.

Only one person would leave beer on her porch, she knew as she made room for it in her small refrigerator. Walking from the kitchen, she pressed her hands together, wringing them without realizing it. Jason had come and found her gone; it was what she wanted, so why did she feel so letdown and disappointed?

Knowing how unfair it was, she still couldn't help comparing Roger to Jason. Everything Roger did was planned and orderly; even after six months he wouldn't think of dropping in unannounced, and he certainly wouldn't litter her porch with a beverage he himself intended to drink. She could depend on Roger to call first for dates, lead the right card in bridge, and be in Banbury the next year, and the next and the next.

With Jason nothing was sure. He acted on his own whims, disturbing her peace of mind at every turn. He himself didn't know where his wandering career would take him, and worse, he seemed to love the uncertainty, seeing it as an adventure, not a trial.

Even as she got ready for bed, the two men filled her thoughts. Remembering Roger's kiss was like recalling a friendly pat on the head; thinking of the way Jason took possession of her mouth agitated her almost as much as his physical presence. His lips were broader than hers, his mouth larger; he'd never had to have four teeth pulled so the orthodontist could make room for the rest. But when he kissed her, it was a perfect meeting, thrilling because it was so right.

After peeling off her pantyhose, she lay on her bed and extended one slender leg toward the ceiling, no longer appalled as she had been as an adolescent by its length. Jason made her love her height, feeling cherished just the way she was for the first time in her life, instead of wishing herself shorter. Absentmindedly she went through her routine exercises, wondering how the evening would have gone if she'd been home when Jason came.

Determined to wear herself out, she did double her usual number of sit-ups and toe touches, then ran in place until her breath came in ragged bursts. When she finally fell into bed, she felt pleased with the trim fitness of her body, but not with the thoughts that kept her wide-eyed and restless. To put herself to sleep, she tried replaying the evening's bridge hands one by one, as much as she could remember of them, but every time she imagined her partner's hand it was held by Jason, not by Roger. Counting sheep wasn't any more successful; they seemed to jump into the lining of his coat before they were properly counted.

Eventually she fell asleep, trying to think of something that didn't remind her of Jason.

## CHAPTER SIX

The day began with chilling winds that pushed a heavy gray cloud cover over the town, and by the time Sara left the bank in late afternoon dusk had turned the threatening sky into a black pall. The cold was refreshing after a full day in the close warmth of the bank, but she rounded the corner on Locust Street at a brisk pace, anxious to reach home before she was caught in a storm. A block from her house she saw the burgundy sports car pull into her driveway, Jason spotting her on the street before he reached her door. He was blocking her approach as she neared the house.

"Am I here ahead of Roger?" he asked.

"Roger isn't coming," she said, not resorting to subterfuge, even though his tone of voice was mildly annoying.

"Good. Then you can come for a ride with me."

"I'm tired, Jason. I'd rather not."

"I'm tired, too. Tired of driving over here and not finding you home. Did you have a nice weekend?"

"Lovely. We really enjoyed going to a bigger city," she said, deliberately arousing his curiosity.

"Oh, what big city was that?" he asked with feigned indifference.

103

"Brattleboro. Oh, by the way, I found the beer. Wouldn't you like to come in for a drink?"

"No. What did you do in Brattleboro?"

"Well, we went to a play in the evening, a musical and really excellent. And we had dinner at Whitney's. They do marvelous things with prime rib. And . . . it's pretty cold out here. Are you sure you won't come in?"

"We're going for a ride, remember?"

"I remember your suggesting it. I don't remember agreeing."

"Get in the car, Sara."

"I thought you wanted to hear about the Christmas shopping Aunt Rachel and I did in Brattleboro."

To mask his relief at the mention of her aunt, he growled threateningly. "Will you get in my car, or do I have to sling you over my shoulder and dump you in it?"

His tone suggested it wasn't an idle threat, so she reluctantly moved to the passenger side and climbed in. The door didn't slam very satisfactorily, even though she felt compelled to put her best effort into it to protest his bossiness. She watched in tight-lipped silence as he maneuvered his long legs into position and started the motor, but secretly she enjoyed the relief that had flickered across his face when she mentioned Aunt Rachel.

Even though their seats were so close that his forearm occasionally brushed the sleeve of her coat, they drove for a while as though the other didn't exist, neither willing to begin a conversation.

"Where are we going?" she finally asked when they'd left Banbury behind them, just a sprinkling of lights in the dark valley.

"Boston."

"Be serious."

"I haven't decided. Anywhere out of your town. It's beginning to get to me."

She repressed an impulse to defend the town, knowing Jason was immune to even its most charming feature: the peaceful village green, a meeting place with slatted wooden benches and a bandstand with gleaming white lattice trim. He was interested only in things he could strip or paint or mold or varnish. He probably didn't even notice the dark gray outline of the picturesque stone fence they were passing, one of many in the wooded valley that marked the boundaries of carefully tended pastureland.

"You must have some destination in mind," she said, feeling hemmed in by the blackness of the sky and the metal shell of the car.

"We might as well drive down Covered Bridge Road," he said, not sounding as though their route were of any importance to him.

The roads in this part of the state meandered without an obvious pattern, curving so as not to dissect fields laid out centuries ago, wandering around clumps of ancient maples, and avoiding low stone walls. After what seemed like an awfully long drive, Jason stopped beside the road a short way from the covered bridge, one of many that still dotted the Vermont countryside. In the darkness this one looked like a stretched-out barn, but the interior was a dark cavern.

Side by side they walked to the protective structure, not touching, glad of the wind shelter when they entered the bridge.

"I love covered bridges," she said, making an effort to sound normal. "Can't you imagine this one sheltering a courting buggy a hundred years ago?"

"They didn't cover it so moonstruck teen-agers could neck undisturbed," he said cynically. "Enclosing bridges was done for economic reasons. It was cheaper to protect the wooden planking than to replace it frequently."

"You certainly know how to take the romance out of things, but I still love this old bridge."

"The top may be old, but it's just decorative today. Look below it, and you'll find new steel I beams set in concrete. The wooden trusses are here only for tourists and Sunday painters."

"You're determined to spoil it for me," she complained.

"No, not spoil," he said, moving behind her. "Just make you see things as they really are."

"It's so dark in here," she said, changing the subject, moving away from him. "A car might not see us."

"There's no traffic tonight, and if a car does come, we'll see the lights and hear it. Even a truck can pass us safely if we stay on this side of the bridge."

"At least don't try to tell me these openings aren't here to serve as windows over the water," she said, walking to a space where the siding was off above waist level.

"I won't say a word about the inside of the bridge needing a light source."

"Thanks a lot!"

With a sudden unexpected move he lifted her up and set her on the ledge of the opening. Her coat and skirt slid upward, so she landed on the rough wood with only her pantyhose protecting her upper thighs.

"Jason! You get me down."

"Enjoy the view," he said teasingly. "You don't need me to get down."

"If I slide off, I'll get splinters!"

"Yes, you might at that, but I'm a whiz with a needle and tweezers."

"You're sadistic! I hate splinters! When I was little and my mother had to dig out one of mine, she'd shut all the doors and windows so the neighbors couldn't hear me screaming."

"You must have been a handful," he said, standing so close that he held her prisoner on the ledge.

"Jason, get me down!"

"Some people never remember the magic word."

"Oh, all right, please."

"Please what?"

"Pretty please with sugar on it get me off this damn splintery ledge."

"My pleasure."

Having ducked under his arm the instant her feet touched ground, she ran to the dark midpoint of the bridge, her sharp heels echoing in the wooden tunnel. Taking advantage of the deeper blackness, she tiptoed to hide beside one of the protruding beams on the side.

"Sara, I know you're there."

Holding her breath, she sensed his presence only a few feet away, but when he passed, she tiptoed as quietly as possible to a spot of concealing darkness on the other side.

"You're playing a dangerous game, Gilman, Sara. When I win at hide-and-seek, I demand a forfeit."

Her giggle betrayed her, and before she could hide again, she was caught.

"My forfeit," he demanded, catching her hand and pulling her to him.

His face was so close she could see the frostiness of his breath in the bitingly cold air. When he lowered his head to brush her lips with his, she backed against a support, evading his kiss, even though she wanted it.

"You can't get away," he said, running his fingers under the hair at the back of her neck.

She felt his kiss all the way down to her numbed toes, and without thinking, she wrapped her arms around his neck, loving the softness of the hair at the nape of his neck.

"How much longer are you going to deprive me?" he asked, the misery in his voice an accusation.

What could she tell him that she hadn't already explained?

"Please take me home," she begged.

He released her and turned to walk back toward the car. Watching her footing, she followed him, her nostrils filled with the damp scent of weathered wood and decaying stubble in the fields. As soon as she left the shelter of the bridge, a flake of snow hit her forehead, melting into a wet trickle.

Jason waited for her beside the car door, large, fluffy snowflakes sticking in his dark hair. She brushed a few away, more from a need to touch him than because the gesture was effective. In fact, the snow was beginning to come down so fast she could see only a few feet ahead.

"Get in the car," Jason said. "Looks like the sky is falling."

"The wet part of it anyway," she said, making a futile attempt to brush the snow off her coat and hair before she got into the vehicle.

Jason carefully negotiated a U-turn, his visibility cut to almost nothing by the increasingly thick curtain of blowing snow.

"It's coming down so hard," she said. "Can you see what's ahead?"

"On the road? Yes, well enough so you don't need to worry. This car handles pretty well under bad driving conditions."

"I'm not worried," she said coolly. "After all, I did live in northern Michigan. We had whiteouts there."

"Well, this isn't quite a whiteout yet, but if we get much snow, the wind is going to create some deep drifts."

He drove with grim concentration, a few times forcing his car through pockets of accumulated snow several inches deep.

"Is the road slippery?" she asked.

His silence told her it was a foolish question.

She felt a glimmer of relief when they turned onto a more heavily traveled blacktop road, but the intensity of the storm was building, making driving extremely hazardous. The lights of the oncoming cars weren't visible until they were nearly on top of them, and the danger of ramming a slower-moving or stalled vehicle in their own lane was increasing by the minute. Jason glanced frequently into the rearview mirror, watching for the approaching headlights of any vehicle behind them that might be traveling faster than he was.

"I'm glad you're driving, not me," she said, knowing that the skill of the driver was crucial in a blizzard and not wanting the responsibility for both their lives. A slight error in judgment could result in a spin, a collision, or a crash into roadside obstacles. In a storm like this, the stately maples along the shoulder became menacing.

They reached the lights of Banbury with a mutual sigh of relief, but several stalled cars made the short trip to her house arduous. Both vehicles proved to be deserted, but Jason felt compelled to stop and check their interiors for stranded motorists before going on. On some streets only one lane was unblocked, and traffic crawled with tedious slowness. The drifts in her driveway, when they reached it, were building fast, but he plowed his way in, preferring to protect his car from snow-blinded drivers on the street.

"This excursion wasn't one of my better ideas," he said, grinning at her now that they were safely off the road. "I didn't expect a storm to build this fast."

She laughed lightly, noticing that snow had covered the windshield the minute he turned off the wipers.

"Well, you'd better come in, I guess."

"You should do that more often."

"What?"

"Laugh. And invite me in. Sometimes you make me feel downright unwelcome."

"Oh, Jason, what am I going to do with you?" She opened the car door with amused exasperation.

"Feed me, I hope. Stay right there. Don't move."

He hurried to her side of the car, the snow dampening his jeans when he ran through a drifted stretch of the drive.

"Grab my neck," he ordered, bending his face near hers.

"You can't carry me!"

"You can't walk in those shoes."

It was true; she'd worn sling pumps open at the heel to work, and wading through the snow in them wouldn't be much more comfortable than walking in stocking feet.

Laughing and protesting, she finally let him carry her up the porch steps and deposit her in the comparatively sheltered area by the front door before he ran back to the car, taking out a paper bag from the trunk after he had closed the door on the passenger side. She entered the house with only her hair damp, but he was soaked to the knees by the heavy, wet snow. Stamping his feet got rid of the loose flakes, but his pants legs clung uncomfortably to his calves.

"Maybe you'd better soak in the bathtub while I throw your jeans in the dryer," she suggested with reservations, suddenly plunged into exactly the kind of situation she feared. Playing house with Jason was like playing with fire, and she knew who'd be the one to get burned.

"I would appreciate a hot shower," he said, shaking the snow off his coat onto the throw rug in her entryway. "I came here directly from work."

"No shower. All I have is a bathtub."

"I'm game if you are."

"Jason! Please don't do that. You may be stranded here, but it doesn't change anything."

"I'll get a room downtown if you prefer."

She hadn't thought ahead that far, but it was obvious that he was stranded; he couldn't drive all the way to Stafford in the storm. The roads would be completely impassable soon if they weren't already.

"I'm afraid you can't," she said regretfully. "The only hotel in town was converted to a senior citizens' home a few years ago. There's a waiting list to get in, and you have to be over sixty. No overnight accommodations are available."

"Maybe the snow will stop, and the plows will go out," he offered helpfully.

The glare she gave him was supposed to be withering,

but again his answering grin told her how much he was enjoying her predicament. She had a houseguest, no matter how unsettling the prospect was.

He hung his coat in her front closet and pushed his paper bag into a back corner of the floor. Sara noticed it but decided not to show her curiosity.

"Leave your jeans outside the bathroom door. I'll throw them in the dryer," she offered. "Towels are in the cabinet in the bathroom. Take your time. I have to think of something to fix for dinner."

"Thanks," he said, disappearing into the bathroom.

She quickly gathered the neat bundle he'd made of his wet pants and socks, rinsing out the latter and throwing them into the dryer immediately because she couldn't possibly supply him with temporary garments. His shoulders were too wide to squeeze into her loosest robe.

If she was resourceful anyplace, it was in the kitchen. She threw together a quiche and made a tossed salad, adding some cheese and strips of leftover ham to make the meal more substantial. She was vigorously shaking her favorite combination of herbs into a bottle of vinegar and oil when she became aware of Jason watching her from the doorway.

"Don't let me interfere," he said, smiling. "I enjoy watching you work."

He filled the doorway, the towel knotted around his waist barely reaching to the middle of his thighs. The dark hair curling over his chest and legs clung damply to his skin, making her want to rub him dry with a towel before he got chilled. His bare white feet made him seem vulnerable, although Sara couldn't have explained why, and she had to fight a crazy urge to mother him.

"I'll see if your jeans are dry," she said, running down the cellar steps before she gave in to the temptation to look at him again.

The legs of his pants were still damp, but his wool crew socks felt dry enough; she'd squeezed them in a towel after washing them out by hand, a chore she felt foolish doing, even though it seemed silly to dry socks without washing them. After resetting the dryer, she impatiently slammed the door, feeling awkward about presenting the man with his socks. He was still lounging in the kitchen, sniffing her dressing, so she sidestepped her awkwardness by laying his socks on a counter near him.

What was wrong with her! She'd helped her mother with the laundry hundreds of times, folding more of her father's and brother's clothes than she cared to remember. She was acting like an addlebrained thirteen-year-old, imagining there was some intimacy in handling a pair of socks.

"Thank you," he said, retrieving his laundry from the counter. "I take it my pants aren't dry."

"Not yet. I gave them a few more minutes in the dryer."

"Well, I'll put on what I have," he said, leaving her to set the kitchen table.

His red plaid flannel shirt hung to the tops of his thighs, and his socks went to midcalf, so there was no reason for Sara to feel so self-conscious with him. Men wore far less on the beach, she reminded herself, trying to keep occupied so she wouldn't let her eyes stray to Jason, dressed as he had been except for the still-damp jeans.

"No linen tablecloth and candlesticks?" he asked with mock disappointment. "I thought you'd at least set up our dinner in the living room."

"You're getting fed, but this isn't a dinner party," she said, annoyed at herself for letting his teasing get to her.

"And I certainly am not a bank president," he said.

"Vice-president." She corrected him irritably, then realized he was only baiting her again.

"May I help do anything?"

"No, everything is ready except the quiche. It needs a little more time in the oven."

"Do you mind if I have one of my beers?"

"I'd be glad to get them out of my refrigerator. Did you have to buy two dozen?"

"I hate running out to the store."

He helped himself to one of the cans cluttering the shelves and door of her refrigerator, popping the tab and taking a long sip.

"You'll get a potbelly, drinking that stuff," she warned him, wanting to punish him for making her aware of his long, tightly muscled legs.

"You hate any situation where you're not fully in control, don't you?" he asked.

Startled by the truthfulness of his observation, she defended herself heatedly. "There's nothing wrong with a woman's knowing what she wants from life."

"That wasn't what I was implying at all," he said, moving closer. "I'm just trying to understand why you deny your own feelings and cling to a life-style instead of living life."

"What I do with my life is none of your business."

"I wish it weren't," he said grimly, his features hardening with regret. "You're the last woman I would have chosen to care about."

"I'll see if your jeans are dry," she said, turning away as if to dismiss him.

"Forget my jeans. You can run away from me, but you can't run away from yourself, Sara."

"You have no right to make judgments about me! I'm not running away because I'm already where I want to be."

"Are you? I know I have no rights with you, and it's driving me up the wall."

He covered the distance between them in two broad steps and captured her in his arms before she could retreat. Sara felt the knobby handle of a drawer press into her hip as he attacked her mouth, drawing the blood to her lips with vindictive force.

113

"You're hurting me," she gasped when he gave her breath to protest.

"What do you think you're doing to me?"

He pressed his fingers against the fleshiness of her buttocks, grinding her against the hardness of his desire. Enraged by the burning sensations shooting through her groin, she fought him, pushing her hands against his chest with no effect.

The strident buzzing of the timer on the stove separated them, and she bent to check the quiche, her hands trembling and her bottom hurting where his fingers had clutched. So angry she could hardly see, she pulled out the pan and banged it against the top of the stove.

"I'm sorry," he said, the words coming so reluctantly that they nearly strangled him.

"You hurt me," she said furiously.

"I said I'm sorry!"

"That doesn't help."

"You are the most rigid, unbending little bitch I've ever met," he said in a rage, blood rushing to his face and staining his high cheekbones with angry splotches of color.

"You just hate it because you've met your match. You can flex your muscles and beat your hairy chest till your teeth fall out, for all I care. I don't want to be in love with a migrant worker!"

"In love, Sara?"

"No!"

"Look at me!"

He caught her shoulders and backed her against the door of the refrigerator, the metal cold through the fine cotton material of her tailored blouse. She turned her face from him, resenting the hold he had on her heart far more than the hands that kept her there.

"Are you in love, Sara?" he repeated in a warm, husky voice that seared her heart.

"It won't work!"

"But it does exist?"

"You should have stayed away. I wanted you to."

"I'm not that strong!"

His lips brushed her hairline, tickling her forehead with tiny kisses, as his hands slowly moved down the ridge of her hipbone. She felt caught in the vortex of a whirlpool, swept wildly into a flurry of sensation. Her rigid control was slipping out of reach as his hands worked a tingling feat of magic on her overly restrained senses.

After releasing the button and zipper of her skirt, he pushed the garment downward, letting it fall in a heap of forest green wool around her feet. Her slippery half slip followed, but she was aware only of him, his face nuzzling her cheek as his hands slipped under the filminess of her pantyhose.

"I hate myself for hurting you," he whispered, gently caressing the cushiony flesh he'd roughly abused just minutes ago.

The contours of her body reshaped themselves against his hard torso, her breasts flattened against his chest as he lifted her against him. Dizzy with yearning, she felt the world shrinking until only the two of them existed, man and woman, lover and loved.

"Will you . . . come with me . . . to your bedroom?" he asked, punctuating every phrase with demanding kisses that trailed from her eager lips down the column of her ivory neck.

The word "no" deserted her; to refuse him now was beyond her. She clung to him with every ounce of her strength as he carried her into the dimness of her room. For an instant she noticed the snow building up against the panes of window glass and the movement of the curtain as the furnace forced warm air into the room. Then Jason lowered her to the bed, switching on the bedside light, and all she could see was him.

His shirt was work-stained with a dab of paint on the collar, and suddenly she resented the cloth that hid him from her sight. With shaky fingers she unbuttoned it, his pleased expression making her heart swell responsively. He helped her then, casting aside his shirt and shuddering when her soft palms moved over his nipples, then downward to slip under the bank of elastic at his waist.

"Let me undress you first," he crooned, kneeling beside her, ritualistically removing each piece of clothing, marveling over every inch of her trembling flesh as it was revealed to his hungry gaze. He delicately traced the outlines of her nipples with the tip of his tongue, as his hands slowly stroked the smooth skin of her abdomen. He sighed with pleasure as the rosy peaks tautened, and Sara caressed the tender skin at his nape, pulling him even closer to her trembling body. She had the peculiar feeling that she was watching another woman who'd taken possession of her body, but she swam along on the currents of desire generated by Jason, removing his socks and touching the top of his foot, caressing his ankle with slender fingers. The immensity of her love for this man made her cherish everything about him, wanting his pleasure so much more than her own. The differences between their bodies, both long and lithe, were miracles to be explored with a sense of wonder. Love was no single feeling, she realized, startled by her own acuteness; it was a blend of warm and wonderful emotions: the infatuation of a young girl, the tenderness of a mature person, the longing of a sensual woman, the excitement of reaching beyond herself. Belonging took on a new meaning as their yearning reached new heights.

She trembled but made no effort to hide it as she slid his shorts down his legs, then fell back on the sheet beside him as the impact of what was happening between them penetrated her consciousness. Her sane inner self questioned the abandonment she felt, but her emotions were totally in control, making even a brief second of separation intolerable.

"Love me," he said, "the way I love you."

Jason knelt over her, his legs pressed against her thighs and hips, caressing her with long, seeking fingers, finding the sensitive spots that made her quiver with expectation. His lips against her skin shot electric shocks of pleasure through her nervous system, and she circled his neck with her arms, pulling his body against hers, squirming not to escape the burden of his weight but to revel in the wonder of being with him. How could she have risked losing him? The prospect of life without this man she loved now seemed so empty and desolate that she shuddered in fear.

Looking into her face, he read the completeness of her need for him and lowered his lips to hers, putting all his own bottled-up love into their joining.

"You're so beautiful," he said in a muffled voice.

"Hold me, love me, Jason."

When he claimed her fully, she arched her back to meet him, caught up in the force that was welding them together. Her throbbing need overrode a stab of pain, hurling her into a deep canyon, whirling her through time and space, joining her to her loved one as they were swept along in a wild give-and-take of pleasure. When at last he shuddered and ceased his rhythmic thrusts, she clung to him with shaking limbs, her love a growing, pulsing emotion that fed on their intimate sharing.

"Are you all right?" Jason's face hovered over hers, beaded with perspiration, so softened by passion and concern he was almost unrecognizable.

"I'm fine," she said, smiling to prove it, knowing it was true, trailing two fingers over his cheek with a feathery touch that affirmed the depth of her love.

He eased the comforter over them, wrapping his legs and arms around her, holding her against him as the pungent perfume of their lovemaking engulfed their senses.

"I adore you," he whispered just as she slipped away from consciousness.

Jason's breathing was soft and regular, but the heaviness of his arm across her breast made her wiggle just enough to rouse him. His eyes opened lazily, and his hand strayed to the mound of flesh his arm had been crushing. His finger traced a circle around the sensitive tip of her breast as his eyes looked into the liquid blueness of hers.

"Love me?" he asked.

"Yes," she admitted gravely, wondering if life would ever again be quite so perfect as it was at that moment. She wanted to stay in bed beside him forever, never again to face the problems that lurked outside her bedroom door. If she could keep Jason here with her, she would ask nothing more from life.

"You are," he said, bending over to kiss her eyelids, "a very slow starter but a very quick learner."

"Don't make this sound like a game," she begged.

"I didn't mean to. I hope you know how much you mean to me."

He pulled her even closer, grazing her cheek with a kiss.

"Are you hungry?" she asked, her ear pressed against his chest detecting a little rumble

"Starved!" he said, smiling. "I skipped lunch to get away sooner this afternoon."

"Dinner's probably ruined."

"I'm not worried."

His kiss was deep and sweet, thrilling because it demanded nothing. She didn't want to get up because it meant the end of their first time together.

"I wish I could freeze this moment and keep it forever," she said wistfully.

"You can't freeze time, but you can re-create it. I do it all the time."

"With wood and plaster."

"Trust me," he whispered into her hair.

His jeans were dry, but so was her quiche. She grated extra cheese on top and rewarmed it while Jason listened to storm reports on the radio.

"There's not a road open between here and Stafford,"

118

he said, unable to disguise a trace of satisfaction in his voice.

"Did you know it was going to storm?"

"I may have heard a weather report driving over."

"Jason, you took an awful chance driving out to the bridge."

"We were never in any danger."

"I've never seen a blizzard start so quickly."

"Do you regret having me stranded here?"

She shook her head, but it wasn't enough for him. He held her against him, tenderly massaging the base of her neck until she melted against him, then tilting her head to rain tiny kisses over her face.

"This has been the best day of my life," he said solemnly, reluctant to free her and break the spell.

The rewarmed quiche was better than she'd expected, still creamy and flavorful, the salad was crisp and tangy with a dash of her dressing, and the coffee tasted strong but not bitter, or so it seemed to Sara and Jason, their palates seasoned by love. They ate crowded together on one side of the small table, feeding each other an occasional bite just for the intimacy it imparted. Laughing at an inopportune moment, she let a drop of salad oil dribble on her chin, and his tongue swished it away, an interruption in their dinner that lasted several minutes.

"Do you want to watch television?" she asked when their midnight supper was cleared away.

"No, I want to make love to you again if you want me to."

His words were blunt, but his eyes were soft and compelling, following her movements like a mountain cat stalking its prey. In spite of all that had passed between them, she felt shy, hesitant to answer him directly.

"I think I'll take a bath," she said, not meeting his gaze.

"You have a great tub; modern ones are usually too short for me."

"I'm sorry I don't have a shower. I plan to have one installed someday."

"Maybe you won't need to."

Avoiding this subject because it reminded her that the future was unresolved, she excused herself, avoiding anything that could ruin this wonderful time with Jason. Standing naked with one toe in the tub of water, she thought for the first time about the broken lock on the bathroom door. Jason was right about needing to call a locksmith, but when he stepped quietly into the room, she wasn't sorry she never had.

"Wash your back?" he asked, smiling down at her, his eyes alight with pleasure.

"I might splash your jeans and get them wet again."

"I planned to take them off."

Trying to fit both their lengths into the tub would have seemed ridiculous if it hadn't been so much fun. The slippery bath water rose above her breasts as he sank down, facing her, and a thick layer of bubbles backed up behind her shoulders. Kneeling in front of her, he soaped a washcloth and ran it carefully over her face, rinsing and patting it dry with a towel lying on the nearby hamper.

His hand moved the cloth briskly over her back and more slowly over her breasts, covering them with rich lather that dissolved slowly. Capturing first one foot and then the other, he separated her toes, sliding a slippery finger between them, making her giggle from more than ticklishness.

"I'll wash your back," she offered.

"No, this is your turn."

After kissing her gently, he rose from the water to dry himself with quick vigorous swipes of the towel. Letting it drop to the floor, he offered her his hand, smiling so warmly that she forgot to be self-conscious about the nudity of her dripping body.

It took him only an instant to find her largest beach towel in the cupboard, but instead of wrapping it around her, he started patting her dry with one end, beginning with her neck and working down the front of her torso, gently blotting every curve until she felt embarrassed by her own eagerness to be in his arms again. Moving to her back, he continued the sweet torture, drying her slowly from shoulders to toes, then winding the towel around her, imprisoning her arms and leading her barefoot into the bedroom.

She watched intrigued as he folded down the comforter, surprised that he'd brought her small kitchen radio to the bedstand. Moving the dial while she stood watching, he found an FM station that played continuous semiclassical music, then turned off the ceiling light, finally slipping the towel from her shoulders and guiding her to the bed. He joined her, pulled the covers over both of them, then lay without moving for so long she wondered if he'd fallen asleep.

"Jason?" she whispered. "Are you awake?"

"Yes. Are you thinking about me?"

"How could I not be!"

She fell on top of him, roughly tweaking his ear to punish him for once again teasing her. They kissed and hugged, playful until Jason began caressing sweet, innocent spots, the skin behind her ear, the hollow of her neck, the base of her spine, slowly arousing her in ways she'd never imagined possible. Fighting his own urgency, he let her sail uncharted seas with his hand firmly on the rudder, pulling her back to dry ground whenever rising swells threatened to engulf her. For a brief instant she felt jealousy rise like bile in her throat, hating the women who had helped him learn to be such a marvelous lover, but the fullness of her feelings for him washed it away. When he took her, love sounds rose instinctively from her throat, swelling and building until her cry hung like a banner in the empty air.

"I have something for you," he whispered when they

both lay exhausted. "Reach your hand down beside the bed. You'll feel a paper bag."

"This?" she asked, lazily tossing it so it rested on the matted expanse of his chest.

"Sit up," he ordered. "I had this cleaned for you."

After peeling the sheet away from her breasts, he reached into the bag and shook out the lovely old paisley shawl, which he draped around her bare shoulders with loving care.

The fringe tickled her breasts, but she pulled it tighter, marveling at how soft the old wool felt on her skin. Rearranging it with gentle hands, he pressed his lips to the edge of the shawl, tasting her breast under the dry strands of edging.

"I can't believe you bought this for me. We were complete strangers at the auction."

"Guilt," he said hoarsely, fingering the rose and blue pattern on her shoulder. "You made me feel I'd just stolen a lollipop from a beguiling little girl. I was afraid you were going to burst into tears."

"I didn't look like that! Anyway, you were a long way from me."

"The shawl seemed like a good way to get closer. I didn't expect a sweet-looking blonde to be a stubborn, hard-nosed Yankee."

"Are you telling me you bought it so you could seduce me that night?"

Her eyes flashed teasingly, and she let the shawl drop to the pillow behind her.

Laughing until he shook, he threw the shawl around her and used it to pull her to him, then kissed her sputtering lips until she laughed.

"You don't really mind," he said, cradling her head on his shoulder, "that I thought you were a beautiful, desirable woman the first time I saw you?"

She answered by lying back, sighing deeply, and slipping her leg across his, clinging to his long body with sleepy satisfaction.

"Thank you for the shawl. It's even lovelier than I remembered it."

"You are so very, very welcome."

They slept long past the morning hour when her unset clock should have rung. The brightness in the room alerted her as soon as she awoke, and she groped over his relaxed form to find her alarm.

"Jason, I have to be at work in twenty minutes!"

"You're going to be late," he said, fingering a lock of her hair that dangled over his face.

The prospect of telling Roger she was late because she'd been making love with Jason late into the night made her giggle, albeit a little nervously.

"I'm never late for work." She hurried out of bed and looked around helplessly for her robe, aware of Jason's eyes drinking in her nudity. "Where is that darn robe?"

"In the bathroom, but look outside, darling. Chances are the snow has the whole town closed down."

The damp snow sticking against the window made it almost impossible to appraise the situation outside, so she hurried, shivering, to the bathroom and wrapped up in her robe. Jason returned her radio to the kitchen counter. Sitting casually by the table, wearing only his shorts, he listened intently to an announcer.

"Don't you ever get cold?" she asked with a trace of irritation, not wanting to be distracted by the lean, pleasing lines of his shoulders and the long, powerful expanse of his legs. His touch was still too fresh in her mind to be able to see any part of him with indifference.

"Listen," he cautioned her. "Schools are closed all over the area. Church rummage sale is canceled. Ladies' aid called off. Snow plows are out, but most secondary roads haven't been plowed yet."

"Roger walks to work," she said grumpily. "He'll be

there to open the bank if there's ten feet of snow blocking the door."

"I'll call and tell him you'll be late," he offered mischievously.

"No!" she protested too vigorously. "I mean, I wouldn't want him to know . . . I mean . . ."

"Okay, tell him your own way." Jason didn't seem concerned one way or the other.

She rushed to get ready, flustered by her lateness and further unnerved because Jason was waiting in her bedroom after she had taken an ultra-fast dip in the tub, watching her dress, silently studying every move she made in a way that upset her composure.

"Your job isn't worth getting into a frenzy," he said pointedly.

"Right now it's the only job I have. I can't afford to lose it."

"You won't get fired for being late on a morning like this. You're going to have a hard time getting there unless you own hip boots. Anyway, I'd like to see you out of the bank." He leaned back against her pillows, fully relaxed and dressed, but inviting her to join him with his eyes.

"To do what?" she asked, becoming more and more agitated as a long run rippled down the length of the hose she'd just put on.

"Look for something that fits your talents. You didn't go to college to be a bank clerk."

"It's a pleasant, respectable job, and I have been looking. Jobs don't grow on trees around here."

"You can quit the bank today."

"Jason, what are you suggesting?" She aimed the torn pantyhose at a wastebasket and, missing, then scooping it up nervously.

"Let me live here for a while. You won't need to worry about expenses."

"For how long?"

Her words hung in the air, cruel because they both knew the answer.

"Until Christmas," she whimpered, hurt by the knowledge that their wonderfully happy interval was over.

"I have a contract . . ."

"Yes, Ohio."

"Come with me."

"And after Ohio?"

"I have to work, Sara. That doesn't mean we can't be together."

"Jason, you don't understand! I live here. I belong here. I can't face move after move after move."

"You belong with me, darling."

He got up and came toward her, but she turned her back and hurried from the room.

"Sara!"

He reached her, catching her hand in his but letting her pull it away.

"Sit down a minute. Please." The pain in his voice was compelling.

She sank to the couch because her legs wouldn't support her, fighting an almost hysterical urge to burst into tears.

"I want you with me, Sara, and you want it, too," he said urgently. "Maybe your life-style is more comfortable than mine, but give me some credit. I don't expect you to live in an attic apartment the way I do now. I can see my place through your eyes, and it looks pretty shabby. I just haven't cared enough lately to look for a better place, but I can afford any kind of home you want."

"I want this one."

"Sara, be reasonable." His voice showed his exasperation. "I can't make a living in Banbury, Vermont. You can't either, if you'd be honest with yourself. You're bored stiff as a bank teller, and you can't tell me they pay you a quarter of what you're worth."

"Money isn't everything."

"I never suggested it was. Think about us, Sara. Tell me you want to be with me."

"Of course I do!" she said, half sobbing now. "I want you here with me!"

She walked to the window to hide her face from him.

"That's just not possible," he said miserably, coming behind her to press her trembling back against him, wrapping her in arms that should have been comforting but weren't.

"I have to leave for work," she said brokenly.

"No, not yet. Come back to bed with me, darling. Let me show you how much I love you."

"That isn't going to resolve anything," she said, pulling away from him. "You're a nomad, a gypsy. You don't even understand what it means to have roots, to belong."

"I don't believe you can belong to a place after only six months," he said with cruel cynicism, anger replacing his thwarted desire.

"My family has been in this valley for centuries."

"A bunch of long-dead ancestors may have their bones here, but your real family's out living meaningful lives, no matter if they are in Hawaii and the Philippines. Those long-gone people are nothing to you, only a excuse to hide behind your spinster aunt's skirts. Well, I hope it's comfortable in this little cocoon you're spinning because there sure as hell isn't room for a man in it."

"Not all men are like you!"

"If you're talking about Roger, forget him. You don't love him, and if you did, it would be your bad luck. He's a mannequin, a prop in this little scene you've created. I didn't have to make love to you to know he's never been in your bed."

"I don't have to listen to this!"

"You sure as hell don't. As soon as I shovel out my car, I'll be gone."

She ran to the security of her bedroom, the one door in her house with a lock that worked properly.

With shaking hands she phoned the bank from her bedroom, telling Roger she felt ill and wasn't coming in.

"I'm here alone so far," he said a little petulantly, not quite understanding why the rest of the staff didn't have his Spartan dedication toward duty, "but I imagine business will be light until the town digs out."

She hung up, realizing he hadn't even asked what was wrong with her.

Lying with her forehead pressed into the pillow, she could hear the town's single old plow clearing her street. Jason must have found the shovel in the garage by her car because the scraping sound of metal on cement was terribly close. She longed to run to him and beg him to stay with her that day; wouldn't it be better to grasp every moment together than to fight and hurt each other?

Her body ached, but the stiffness left by their lovemaking was the least of her pain. Maybe her lie about being sick had become reality; perhaps she really did have an early-winter virus. Certainly her head ached unmercifully, and her stomach was churning.

The last thing she heard before succumbing to the drug of sleep was Jason's car backing out of her driveway. It never occurred to her to wonder whether he'd cleared the way for her car, too. He had, but she didn't know it for a while. A flash fever kept her in bed for most of Monday, and Tuesday Roger, becoming more sympathetic on hearing her symptoms, convinced her to rest at home instead of coming to work. The day before Thanksgiving came, and Jason hadn't called, not once.

## CHAPTER SEVEN

She was proud, in a gloomy sort of way, of the four fragrant pies, two mincemeat and two pumpkin, cooling on her kitchen counter. They were her contribution to Aunt Rachel's traditional Thanksgiving dinner, but their sweet spiciness didn't make her mouth water in anticipation of the huge feast awaiting her. The only reason she didn't beg off was that the prospect of being home alone all day thinking about Jason was too depressing to contemplate.

To give him credit, Roger had offered to miss his family's large gathering and keep her company if she was still sick, but it was a sacrifice she couldn't let him make. Not only was she perfectly healthy again, but she suspected her twenty-four-hour flu had been an unconscious excuse to hide at home. Why was it that she never got sick when she was happy? She'd never been sick for a party, but she had been known to miss exams, dentist appointments, and spring housecleaning.

Feeling like a sorry specimen, she started dressing for the occasion, ending up in her navy blazer and light gray wool skirt with a white blouse stiffly pleated in front. She was appropriately dressed for a job interview or a day of work at the bank, but she looked about as festive as last

128

year's Christmas tree. Eyeing her red dress dejectedly, she decided not to change; this was Aunt Rachel's big party. Let her be the one to shine. Sara would just blend in with the furniture and help out in the kitchen. She could shed her jacket and wear an apron from her great-aunt's huge collection of frilly and practical cover-ups. Rachel was the only woman she knew who not only owned nearly a hundred aprons but ironed them and wore them regularly. No one really knew what the sprightly lady's wardrobe contained because at school she covered up with smocks in a variety of patterns, ranging from lavender and yellow stripes to red sailboats on a sea of blue, firmly believing that children liked their teacher to look cheerful.

The snow was melting, the slush in the streets turning gray while joyfully constructed snowmen drooped and dripped in every yard where children played. Actually the youthful population of Banbury was fairly small, younger families finding the job market too restrictive. The schools largely drew upon children from farm families, and the enrollment was dropping a little every year.

The last thing Sara did before leaving was turn off the radio in the middle of a dire-sounding weather forecast. Winter was coming early, and holiday travelers were warned about worsening weather conditions later in the day. Fortunately Sara could ignore the warnings; she wouldn't be far from home today.

Sara loaded the pies into her car, forced to drive the short distance because there was no way she could walk carrying four pie plates filled to the brim. Arriving early, she saw only one car in her great-aunt's double driveway, but she parked on the street so no one would block her. She recognized the first car there as belonging to her aunt's longtime friend and fellow teacher Maida Graham; she'd obviously come early to volunteer her help in preparing the meal. Once inside, Sara found Aunt Rachel so well organized that her helpers served mainly as cheerleaders, heaping well-deserved appreciation on their hostess.

Maida was as tall as Sara, but big-boned and stocky, her physical traits emphasized by her hearty sense of humor and a zest for life that matched Rachel's. Sara thought, not for the first time, that single women seemed to thrive in Vermont, developing strong personalities and independent modes of living with no trace of regret or self-pity. Young as she was, she enjoyed the easy comradeship of her great-aunt's friends, who in turn accepted her with an unaffected friendliness lacking in some of the younger town residents.

The dining table, doubled in size by removable leaves, extended through the alcove from the dining room into the living room. Sara counted places set for twenty, her aunt's prized set of Haviland china complete to the last bone dish and butter pat. Aunt Rachel served this meal in the best Victorian tradition, which meant a special dish for every food on the menu: a cut-glass holder for celery, a silver-plated candy dish, a castor set with glass condiment jars, a gravy boat, a soup tureen, platters in half a dozen sizes, and matching Haviland serving dishes for everything from applesauce to yams.

Sara admired the eloquently set table as a work of art, knowing well the skill it took to orchestrate such a large banquet. Every dish should come to the guests piping hot, and foods served cold should be put on the table in frosty dishes; knowing her aunt, that's how it would be. She could accomplish a like production herself with the help of chefs, busboys, and waitresses, but she marveled at how her aunt did it on her own with no time off from school. In spite of all the obvious hard work, she appeared as fresh as the laboriously ironed linen cloth on the table.

"Who's coming?" Sara asked, cornering her great-aunt as she basted a huge golden brown turkey in one of her very modern double ovens.

"Oh, mostly the usual people, dear. I have so much to

130

do yet, would you mind being my hostess? Just have everyone leave his or her coat in the blue bedroom, and, Maida, you can bring any edible contributions in here to me. I always tell my guests not to bring a thing, but they never listen. We'll probably have enough food for an army."

And you'll be out tonight, delivering boxes of leftovers, begging people who really need the food to help you out by accepting the overflow, Sara thought, smiling. It hadn't taken her long to get her great-aunt's number, and she adored her for her openhanded generosity.

The Willards, a retired couple who were alone since their only son had moved to California, arrived first, The baked ham they presented would feed a family for a month, and Mr. Willard proudly handed Sara several bottles of wine with interesting foreign labels.

Some of the guests, especially those who taught with her great-aunt, Sara knew well, but several were strangers, including Colonel Barnham, a retired army man whose dour expression brightened considerably when Rachel ducked out of the kitchen for a moment to greet him in person.

Mentally tabulating the guests who'd arrived, Sara couldn't find a person to fill the twentieth place at the table. Yet it would be completely unlike Rachel to miscount. Her inaccuracies with numbers were strictly confined to her checkbook; she could instantly recall how many students were in her building and how many buttons decorated the front of her mauve silk dress.

"There seems to be one person late," Sara reported in the kitchen when the doorbell hadn't sounded for a reasonable interval.

"Oh, no, dear. He's not late. I gave him a little later time. I always like my star guest to arrive last."

"Your star guest, Aunt Rachel?" Sara asked suspiciously.

"Mr. Marsh, dear. He graciously consented to join us, and I can't tell you how excited I am. Betsy visited the

131

General Dana house last summer, and absolutely everyone has heard all about it. I'm so thrilled that he's joining us."

"Aunt Rachel, is that the only reason you invited him, because he's well known for his restorations?"

She tried not to sound angry, but six months of living in Banbury had taught her that matchmaking was one of her aunt's favorite hobbies. There was no way her relative could know that she was much too late with her well-intentioned scheme. The principal players were already hopelessly, painfully attracted, and her invitation was going to cause a lot of awkwardness, especially for Sara.

"Of course, that's not the only reason," her aunt protested. "Mr. Marsh is a wonderful man. I enjoyed meeting him so much I want my friends to get to know him. I hope you're not cross with me, dear. I did think that the two of you were friends."

"Aunt Rachel, you shouldn't—"

"Oh, there's the bell, and you're not doing your job," her great-aunt said, rebuking her lightly. "Maida will swish him away to the coatroom before you have a chance to greet him."

Sara looked longingly at the kitchen door that led to her aunt's tidy backyard, more than a little tempted to dash out without her coat and make a beeline for home, but her stubbornness asserted itself. If Jason wanted a public confrontation after not calling, not talking to her since their angry parting, he'd get more than he'd bargained for. Visibly squaring her shoulders, she marched out to face the man who hadn't been out of her thoughts since the winter's first blizzard.

Maida had him well in hand, guiding him around the milling circle of guests without even allowing him to dispose of his coat. Her aunt's friend had a competitive spirit, it seemed, snagging the guest of honor and appropriating the pleasure of introducing him.

Sara tried not to notice the way he dominated the gathering, moving with an inborn grace over the rose design of the carpet, avoiding the imaginatively grouped but none too safely placed plant stands, occasional tables, knick-knack shelves, and other obstacles that were part of her aunt's ornate Victorian parlor. When he leaned forward to take the hand of an elderly woman sitting on the gray patterned horsehair love seat, his gesture was so courtly he looked as if he'd kiss the lady's hand. The smiles that followed his circuit of the room certainly justified Rachel's belief that he'd be the hit of the party.

Smiling none too pleasantly herself, Sara decided she'd make the rules for this game. As her aunt's cohostess she'd choose her own dinner companion. The guests were equally divided between single and married people, and the only one who might conceivably be called an eligible bachelor was Colonel Barnham. Tall, lean, and virile-looking, his nearly hairless head giving him a granitelike countenance, he wasn't at all unattractive. Aunt Rachel may have outsmarted herself this time, Sara thought grimly.

Waiting until after Jason had met the colonel and moved on to the next group, she quickly engaged the ex-military man in the kind of conversation her father carried on so skillfully, ignoring the fact that Jason was only a few paces away. In only moments she had the colonel telling her far more than name, rank, and serial number; she had made enough brief comparisons between his military experiences and her father's to convince him they were brother and sister in arms. This man was going to escort her to dinner and sit beside her, foiling her great-aunt's matchmaking plan. Eat your heart out, Aunt Rachel, she thought. This was one scheme that was going to backfire.

Wine was passed around by the group's official connoisseur, Mr. Willard, and Sara wondered if the wine Jason had brought for Thanksgiving would end up as cooking sherry or make the grade as a table wine. Remembering the fine vintage she'd served to Roger, she suspected the latter would be the case.

Several times she was conscious of Jason's stare, but she refused to do more than nod impersonally. Somehow he'd freed himself of both his coat and Maida, only to be cornered by Betsy, who was obviously thrilled to be talking about *the* house with *the* man. Sara smiled, charming the colonel even more, though she'd lost the gist of their conversation and was having a hard time making her comments at the right time.

I hate what I'm doing, she thought miserably. She liked people too well to play silly little games, and she'd much rather turn the colonel over to Rachel, who obviously fascinated him in a much more substantial way than Sara did. She was deliberately flattering his ego, a ploy that worked only because she was young and her great-aunt was stuck in the kitchen.

Her conscience got the best of her, and she suggested that Rachel might need help carrying the heavy soup tureen to the table. The Army obviously hadn't taught the colonel not to volunteer; he raced to the kitchen with an eagerness that at least put Sara's conscience at ease.

She swallowed the last of the sparkling white wine in her glass and tried to spot another likely-looking dinner partner, deciding she'd have to settle for Mr. Willard since husbands and wives certainly wouldn't be seated next to each other. Before she could compliment him on what she hoped was the wine he'd brought, Rachel came into the room and called for a moment's silence.

"Listen, everyone," she trilled, "my class worked so exceptionally hard making Thanksgiving place markers, I just had to promise I'd use some of them on my dinner table today. So everyone has a special name card, and you all can find your places by looking for yours."

Outmaneuvered! Sara was exasperated but unable to be truly angry at her great-aunt. The name cards had not been on the table when she'd last looked at it. Rachel had delayed putting them out until it was too late for her niece to switch them. Sara knew without looking that Jason would be seated beside her.

"Well, Miss Gilman, we seem to be sitting together," Jason said formally, pulling out her chair and waiting for her to be seated.

She couldn't tell by his neutral tone of voice whether he was angry or amused.

"When did my aunt invite you?" she asked, not trying to hide her agitation.

"The day after I met her, I believe it was."

He pushed in her chair with automatic courtesy, then turned to say a few words to the guest on his other side. She was seated at the far end of the table closest to the kitchen with her great-aunt on her left; directly across from her on Rachel's left was Colonel Barnham. Judging by the admiring attentiveness the colonel was bestowing on Rachel, Sara would have to talk to Jason or sulk in silence. At the moment she was leaning toward the latter. Let Jason brag about his wonderful work to Mrs. Willard or Betsy, the two females who occupied chairs beside and facing him; she'd heard too much about it already.

Rachel's French onion soup brought raves from her guests, but Sara barely tasted what she was eating. Jason's knee seemed to stick out at a right angle from his chair, and she raged inwardly because he knew her leg couldn't evade it without bumping into her great-aunt.

"You could have canceled out of this," she whispered when her aunt went into the kitchen for a minute, attended by the more than helpful colonel.

"Why would I want to do that?" he asked, grinning. "If the rest of the dinner is as good as the soup, I'd say I've fallen into a good thing."

"Move your knee!" she said between closed teeth, pushing at it with her hand under the overhang of the table-cloth.

"Careful," he said, leaning close to her ear. "Someone might think you were trying to get fresh."

The carving of the turkey was a ritual her aunt enjoyed, and not surprisingly the colonel was given the honor of advancing to the head of the table to wield the razor-sharp knife and spearlike fork while several other guests carried in the side dishes from the kitchen.

"I should be helping," Sara protested to her aunt, but she was waved off impatiently. Rachel didn't want her to waste time waiting table when she was supposed to be charming Jason.

Plates were passed clockwise the whole circumference of the table, so Sara ended up with the first portion of turkey. After Jason received his, she fervently wished they had been the last served so he could have been kept busy passing plates. His hand, which seemed to be resting on his lap, was actually clasping her knee, his fingers caressing the nylon surface with a familiarity that made her cheeks burn.

"Stop," she ordered, leaning close to his ear, but he pretended not to hear, turning to Betsy to make a comment about Rachel's lovely old sideboard.

Two can play this game, she thought angrily, knowing full well that she was at his mercy. No one could see a thing under the table, thanks to the generous width of Rachel's cloth, and the colonel was slicing the bird with such poky precision that not even half the guests had been served.

Seething with anger, Sara dug her nails into the top of Jason's hand, pressing down with a strength born of indignation. How dare he fondle her knee at her aunt's Thanksgiving dinner?

He endured her clawing attack for several moments, finishing what he was saying to his neighbor, then turned, smiling, to her, speaking with such a pleasant expression no one would dream she was hurting him.

"I suggest," he said in a low voice, "that you stop that."

"I will if you get your hand away from my knee."

She glanced at the colonel, reassured that he was trying too hard to show off his carving expertise to notice the interplay at her corner of the table. Her more alert aunt was busy for a moment in the kitchen.

She withdrew her nails but nearly cried out when Jason's hand snaked upward and rested heavily between her thighs.

"Don't you agree, Sara?" Betsy leaned forward, her gently lined face peering somewhat nearsightedly past Jason.

"I'm—I'm afraid I didn't hear what you said, Betsy."

Her legs trembled as Jason punished her, his hard fingers squeezing, then caressing the soft, vulnerable flesh of her inner thigh. Then, to her immense relief, he had to stop. Heavy dishes of steaming mashed potatoes, oyster dressing, candied yams, cranberry sauce, buttery corn, thick golden gravy, and molded salad started circling the table, requiring two-handed participation by everyone. Platters of maple-glazed ham, walnut bread, homemade yeast rolls, and relishes followed, tempting them all to help themselves to generous servings. Sara filled her plate with little dabs of almost everything, but she would gladly have left the table that moment to get away from Jason's mocking attention. He insisted she taste his yam because there was none on her plate, giving her the choice of accepting a bit from his fork or making a scene, enjoying the embarrassment he was causing her.

The meal progressed through the courses, ending with her pies, her great-aunt's praises of her baking echoed by others, but not by Jason.

"I take it you don't like my pie," she said softly when he pushed away half of his wedge of mincemeat.

"It's delicious, but I feel like a goose being force-fed for Christmas dinner," he whispered confidentially.

"No one forced you to come," she said, defending her

great-aunt's orgy, even though she felt uncomfortably full herself.

"Rachel, you're fired," Jason said loudly as people began to leave the table.

Her great-aunt looked a little startled but smiled sweetly.

"Sara and I are handling the cleanup. You deserve to sit down, take your shoes off, and relax."

"Oh, no," Rachel protested, but she finally had met her match in Jason.

Once the dishes had been carried into the kitchen by a willing crew of table clearers, Jason declared the kitchen to be his absolute domain, permitting no one to enter except his unwilling assistant, Sara. She found a frilly blue apron and exchanged it for her blazer, kicking off her shoes with ill-concealed misgivings. Of course, she'd expected to help clean up, but she hadn't bargained for a closed door that made her Jason's virtual prisoner. Her aunt left them alone so she could steer her overfed guests into nonstrenuous afternoon activities like bridge, backgammon, and book discussions, although even these were more effort than some of her drowsy dinner guests wanted.

"Why did you do this?" Sara asked angrily when they were alone, the conversation of the others only a low din beyond the door Jason had shut.

"We're twenty years or more younger than any of the others. It just seemed a kind thing to do. Anyway, I have to loosen my belt and move around or I'll burst."

"I'm not talking about doing dishes. Why did you come here? You knew I'd probably be here."

"I'm not exactly starting a scandal by doing dishes with you. Your aunt is hardly subtle about nudging me in your direction. I'm making her day a success, being closeted here in the kitchen with you."

He tied a red-striped apron of Rachel's around his waist, the gay feminine ruffles contrasting with the austere brown worsted vest of his suit. His shoulders looked

138

broader now that he'd stripped down to shirt sleeves, the pale cream cotton of his shirt making him look more swarthy. Rolling his cuffs up to his elbows, he surveyed the kitchen clutter.

"It would serve you right if I went home," she said teasingly. "I'll bet you haven't done this many dishes in your life."

"Wrong. My mother went on a equality kick once. She made up a schedule for my sisters and me, so we'd all have to take a turn setting, clearing, washing, and drying. Whenever it was my turn to work with one of them, I whistled loudly the whole time, off key, the same tune. Finally my sisters threw me out of the kitchen because I got on their nerves so much. When we got a dishwasher, I never even had to load it."

"You're unscrupulous!"

"I was when it came to getting out of doing dishes when I was ten or so."

"Do you think you can whistle me into doing all the work?"

"I doubt it."

"I think you and Aunt Rachel both are playing games with me."

"Oh, no, I'm not playing. After three nights without you I feel like I'm being fried on a hot griddle."

He was going to kiss her; she knew it and warned herself to stop him, but her defenses were unreliable. In slow motion he bent his head, his breath warm on her cheek, his eyelashes tickling her lids. His open mouth surrounded hers in a kiss so demanding she felt shock waves down her spine. She tried to freeze him out, willing her lips to become granite and her heart polar ice, but his persistence made her knees rubbery and her will gelatinous. With a sharp murmur of longing, she clutched at him, reveling in the firmness of his back under her hands and the hard swelling under his apron.

"I'v never kissed a man in ruffles before," she said weakly, sure he ached for her as much as she did for him.

"Can we go back to your house?" he asked, his voice muffled as he held her tightly against him, urgently communicating his need.

"You've made sure we can't! We have to do these darn dishes."

"Oh." He groaned. "Well, we can throw them in the dishwasher and leave."

He surveyed the ruins of the Thanksgiving feast with frowning displeasure.

"There's at least three or four loads here. We'll have to do most of them by hand," she told him, not sure how she felt about the chore he'd insisted on doing.

"Great!" he said, picking up a sticky gravy ladle as if it might bite him.

"Blame your own big mouth," she said, pressing two fingers against the lips that were dangerously close to hers again as he threw aside the utensil. Trying to break the spell between them, she nipped at his lower lip.

"Ow! You're going to end up in big trouble," he said, going along with her attempt to surface from their heavy mood, showing his teeth in mock ferocity.

"If you're washing dishes, you might want to take off your tie," she said.

"I'm not washing!"

"You're the volunteer."

"This might be the best time to confirm that woman's place is in the kitchen."

"I'll scream!"

"I'll compromise," he said, grinning. "You organize this mess and load the dishwasher. I'll start scrubbing pans."

"How are you two coming along?" Rachel's head poked around the corner of the door to the dining room, beaming at the two of them with the same benevolence she displayed when her first graders nicely cleaned their desks.

140

"Fine, no problem," Jason said enthusiastically.

"I feel a little guilty, just sitting while you two clean up this awful mess all by yourselves."

"You've done your share, Aunt Rachel. Jason assures me he's a great dishwasher."

"Well, if you're sure . . ."

She started to lift a stack of dessert plates.

"If you lift one finger in this kitchen, I'll spank you," Jason threatened with mock severity.

Aunt Rachel flushed crimson, whether from pleasure or embarrassment, Sara wasn't sure. Did the older woman look just a little ashamed of herself for matchmaking her niece's child with such a brutal, forceful man? The little smirk on her great-aunt's face belied any possibility of a guilty conscience. She looked like one of her six-year-olds caught drawing naughty pictures on the chalk board.

"There's more to that woman than lavender and lace," Jason said when they were alone again. "If that's the stuff women are made of in your family, our daughter will be a little tiger."

His comment made Sara more rattled than the pans she was noisily stacking, so conscious of his presence that she had to clutch her hands into tight fists to keep from hitting him, pounding him, touching him. Her body chemistry must be running amuck; she'd never in her life reacted so violently to anyone.

"Don't take it out on the pans," he said softly, taking her in his arms again and kissing her lightly.

His hand rested on one breast, motionless on top of her blouse, feeling the swell and hardening under his palm. Then he cupped her other breast and pushed both closer together. For a moment she wore her longing on her face, the bitter yearning making her vision cloud and her temple throb.

"I want you," he said.

"Don't kiss me again," she begged, putting her hands on top of his.

141

"I won't kiss you here if you won't scratch me again."

He showed her his hand, little red raw marks visible in several places.

"You started it!"

"Because I was dying to touch you."

"I—I'm sorry I scratched so hard."

Guilt and tenderness made her take his hand in hers and kiss it lightly, pressing the sore spots against her cheek.

"I feel like a yo-yo," she said, "hurtling out into space, then being jerked back again."

"That's not so bad, if you always come back to my hand."

The same inner prompting made them both begin working with energetic haste, tackling the gigantic stacks of dirty dishes with determination. Eventually they made headway, the dishwasher overheating the kitchen until they were forced to open the back door to cool off.

"Where do all these dishes go?" Jason asked, gesturing at the setting for twenty now restored to gleaming cleanliness.

"Top shelf. Even you may need the stepladder to reach it, I think. They made ceilings high in these old houses."

"You climb up, and I'll hand the dishes to you. You're probably a better stacker than I am."

By trial and error Sara managed to fit the gleaming pile of china into the meager space allowed for it, asking at last for the final piece, a heavy covered vegetable dish. Jason handed it to her with one hand and slid the other hand up her leg to pat her thigh.

"Jason! You'll make me drop this dish."

"I want you to drop everything for me."

The moment she managed to slide the dish onto the shelf, he lifted her off the ladder, holding her thighs in the steel band of his arms. Thrown off-balance, she clutched at his neck, grasping it first to save herself from toppling and then because it felt so right.

"Let me love you," he said, sighing against her.

He let her slide to the floor through the circle of his arms, taking her chin in his hand to study the agony of indecision on her face.

"Today? Tomorrow? Forever?" she whispered.

The question wasn't for him; it was the one she herself had to deal with. She loved him desperately, wanting him with all her being, but Christmas loomed ahead like Armageddon, and she was being torn into ribbons by his love. Was wanting him enough for today? Didn't they have to have a goal, a way of sharing their future? He would leave, and she couldn't follow.

"Can you face the future without me?" he asked, searching her face for some sign of hope.

"I'm frightened that I may have to."

"Sara, you're not a vegetable. You can't grow roots and spend the rest of your life bobbing in the breeze and looking at an empty sky. You belong wherever I am. Admit it."

"I can't leave here. I can't follow you back and forth across the country, never knowing where I'll be next year or the next or the next."

"You don't want to leave your safe little shell."

"I don't want your kind of life."

"Live for today then. Forget about the future, and come back to your house with me."

She could only shake her head, numbed by the hopelessness of their feelings for each other.

"At least talk to me about it!"

"Talk or listen to your arguments?"

"Talk!" he said furiously. "I'll get our coats, and we'll walk until we come to some kind of understanding. Come say good-bye to your aunt. And smile. You look like you're going to bawl."

# CHAPTER EIGHT

The streets were deserted, the strong cold wind discouraging after-dinner walkers. Although the sidewalks were clear, the slush piled up against the curbs had frozen solid, making walking hazardous in spots. Leaving their cars parked by Rachel's house, they walked in silence to Sara's, where Jason waited outside for the few moments it took her to change into leather boots that clung protectively to the length of her calves. Without putting it into words, both knew why he wasn't coming inside.

"Would you like to walk through the churchyard?" she asked, joining him on the sidewalk, a little breathless from rushing.

"Whatever you like," he answered indifferently.

They walked side by side but apart, two people together but alone with their separate thoughts. Because what they wanted to say was so important, neither wanted to begin. What remained unsaid couldn't be regretted.

The business district was closed down for the holiday; not even the gas station was open for customers. Jason turned up his overcoat collar as a windshield, and Sara wrapped her scarf more securely around her neck. The wind whipped at their faces, but neither seemed to notice.

"Careful, it's slippery here," he warned, automatically reaching out for her arm and not releasing it when they'd passed the icy patch.

Main Street wound through town, bringing them to the outskirts, where the village church stood as a sentinel over a burial ground that was old when farmers still drove in for services in horse-pulled wagons. The stormy darkness of the sky robbed the small cemetery of any charm it possessed, but Sara felt drawn to its bleakness, entering it through a wooden gate set in weathered stonework. The snow that spotted the withered grass had melted and frozen again, lying in grainy, soiled patches around markers chiseled on austere stone slabs.

"Not a very cheerful place," Jason commented glumly.

"No, but it's very old, very historical. Here's my favorite plot," Sara said dully, walking up to a row of similar stone markers.

"Abigail, wife of Joshua." Jason read the heavily weathered lettering. "And here's Patience, wife of Joshua. And Elisabeth, another wife of Joshua. He certainly wore out his wives. Why is it your favorite?"

"I guess favorite is the wrong word. It just touches me because it's so sad. See how young the first two were. They may have died in childbirth. I can't help wondering what their thoughts were, how they felt about life."

"Women didn't have much time to sit around being philosophical in those days. Just putting a meal on the table was a day's work."

"You always think of the practical things," she said accusingly.

"Is that so bad? I wish I could convince you to be practical. Maybe then you'd see that we want the same thing: each other."

She walked away, weaving her way around several plots enclosed by old iron fencing, not looking behind to see if Jason followed. Stung by his whole attitude, she didn't

145

point out the resting place of a Civil War soldier or show him where her own ancestors lay.

Walking was hazardous, but Sara moved rapidly, needing to burn off her frustration. The stone wall dipped unevenly in spots where segments had crumbled and not been replaced. She stepped over an especially low section hidden behind a giant maple and made her way to a rough pathway running behind the cemetery. Beyond it was a ridge nearly blocked by trees and a fast-flowing stream. When Jason caught up with her, he grasped her arm, slowing her against her will. The trail was too narrow for two, so he followed right behind her until they reached a weathered wooden footbridge crossing the waterway.

"Don't race ahead," he said. "The sky looks pretty ominous."

"I'm not ready to turn back."

"All right, we'll stay here awhile."

He put his arm around her shoulders, shivering with her as the wind assaulted them with new force. A few hard pellets of snow bombarded the wooden planking, sticking there like powdered sugar sprinkled on a cake.

"I don't know how I can leave without you," he said, holding her against his side, his eyes in profile hooded.

"Don't leave, Jason. There are houses everywhere. You can work here."

"Sara, please understand. The kind of work I do is too specialized. I can't stay in Banbury."

"And I can't leave," she said miserably.

"As my wife you wouldn't need to be afraid of new places. You'd have me to help you adjust to them."

He stuck his gloves in his pocket, took her face in his hands, and kissed her with a tenderness that made her heart contract.

"Marry me, Sara. Please."

"I want to, Jason, but—"

"But?"

"We have to live in one place; we have to belong. I won't

146

force my children to change from school to school, city to city, always being outsiders."

"Our children will love new experiences. They'll learn to survive in any situation."

"No. Jason, you're asking me to sacrifice the way of life I love, but you're not willing to change yourself."

"Are you calling me selfish?"

"Maybe. I don't know."

"Sara, you can't honestly believe it will make either of us happy if I give up my career. I can't go to work in a bank. I've worked for years to get where I am. What I do with historic buildings no one else can do as well as I do. Are you really asking me to give it up?"

"No, you can't. I understand that; but I know I'll never be a migrant, a nomad who doesn't belong anywhere, and I won't have children if they have to live that way."

As she turned away from him into the wind, heavier gusts of snow pelted against her face, stinging her skin but hardly noticed in her agitation.

"Not all children retreat into a little shell when they're exposed to the real world," he argued angrily. "Your brother joined the Navy; he must have thrived on your parents' travels."

"I'm not my brother!"

"But you're using nonexistent children as an excuse to hide from life."

"I am not. I have as much right as you do to choose the way I live."

"What is it about this place that has its clutches into you? You could exchange Banbury for one of a thousand other New England villages and not know the difference."

"You're talking about buildings; I'm talking about people."

"As far as I can see, all your friends are old enough to be your parents. Except Roger. Does Roger come into this?"

She shook her head, not wanting to talk about Roger.

"Maybe he does," Jason said scornfully, turning away from her to stare at the shallow water flowing over rocks below the bridge. "If Roger didn't exist, you'd make him up, just like you've created a quaint little village in your imagination."

"What do you mean?" She felt blood rushing to her face as her anger built.

"Banbury. It's an illusion. What it is and what you think it is are two different things. You're living in a fairy tale, Sara, complete with your own version of Prince Charming. Even the name of the place is romantic nonsense. Ride a cockhorse to Banbury Cross."

"If that's what you think, just leave me alone. It's what I wanted you to do from the beginning."

"Did you? I wonder."

She turned away furiously and ran across the slippery boards of the bridge. The leather-clad soles of her feet slid over the snow-flecked wood and sent her sprawling, too mortified at first even to notice whether she was injured.

"Darling, let me help you," he begged, cradling her in his arms as he knelt beside her.

"I'm not hurt," she said, choking back tears of rage.

Slowly he helped her to her feet, full of concern when she winced in pain.

"My ankle."

"Don't try to put your weight on it."

"No, it's okay. Just twisted, I think."

"Lean on me," he ordered.

Stubbornly she refused, starting down the path on her own, even though daggers of pain stabbed at her ankle.

"Your ankle hurts like hell, I'll bet," he said behind her. "Your stubbornness is going to get you in real trouble someday, Gilman, Sara."

"Oh, leave me alone," she said, her voice muffled by the tears she was choking back.

"Is that your solution to everything? Just stalk off and hide alone in a corner?"

"You make me so mad!"

She turned and faced him furiously, her cheeks chapping as hot bitter tears coursed down them.

"Oh, Sara."

Wrapped in his arms, she sobbed against him as the snow came down with increasing density.

"I think we'd better get out of this weather while we can still see where we're going," he said softly.

Groping in her purse for a tissue, she felt the icy wind buffet her face, making it sting and burn.

He led with a firm grasp on her hand, relying on the path to lead him back toward the church since visibility was getting poorer and poorer. When Sara stumbled on her throbbing ankle, he walked more slowly, his shoulders tight with tension and his eyes squinting into the curtain of snow.

Snow was beating against the grave markers, making the solitude of the burial ground seem as desolate as outer space. Carefully they picked their way between protruding stone monuments, more than half-blinded by the snow.

"Let's check the church," he shouted over the wind.

The latch on the door of the small stone church made a metallic clicking noise as Jason released it, relieved that there was no lock to bar the way. Inside, the aroma of melted wax and steam-heated air enveloped them, inviting them to find sanctuary there.

Sara gave up all pretense of walking normally, hobbled to an ushers' bench along the back wall, and sank down with relief. She could feel her ankle swelling inside her boot, but she didn't want Jason to know how bad it was.

He knelt at her feet, bringing a protest from her that he ignored, unzipping her boot down the length of her calf and pulling it gently over her heel.

"Whew! And you walked here on that ankle." His tone was reproving but concerned.

When he probed the swelling with gentle fingers, she couldn't help yelping a little.

149

"Sorry. It's sprained probably," he said, pushing her boot back onto her foot but not trying to force the zipper up over the swelling. "I'll go get my car and drive you home."

"It's snowing so hard you might get lost," she warned. "People walk out in blizzards and die only feet from their own homes."

"Are you worried about me, Sara?"

She didn't answer, standing, instead, and limping to one of the high arched windows that lined the two side walls of the nave. Outside, she couldn't see even the outlines of the tombstones as wildly blowing snow whipped against the glass.

"You shouldn't stand on your ankle," he said, running his fingers over her cheek.

"Stay with me until the snow stops blowing," she urged.

"I will if you'll sit down."

He guided her to the nearest seat, a dark high-backed pew that extended halfway across the church, its counterpart standing on the other side of the center aisle. The wood had the patina that only age can give it, glowing but muted by generations of use. She slid down a ways on the smooth seat, making room for him to sit beside her, pulled off her gloves and tucked them in a pocket.

His hand covered hers, surprisingly warm on her icy fingers, stroking the back of her hand absentmindedly as he stared at the simple altar in the sanctuary.

"I wish I understood," he said almost to himself.

Her hand tensed under his, and he took it palm to palm and intertwined their fingers, rubbing his thumb caressingly over the veins of her wrist. A sense of peace slowly crept over her, one she didn't want to shatter by speaking.

"Think how many words have poured out from that pulpit over the years," he said. "I wonder how many really took root and changed the lives of the hearers."

"Words can be powerful," she said.

"Feelings are stronger."

150

He wasn't talking about sermons and congregations now.

"I hear your words," he said slowly, "but they contradict the other signals you're sending me. I think you want me as much as I want you. I think you love me."

"I do," she said hoarsely.

"Then why does it have to be your way or nothing?"

"That's not what I'm asking. I will leave Banbury, but not to be dragged from place to place like part of your baggage for the rest of my life."

"You don't think we can have a comfortable life unless we settle down forever in one place?"

His words condemned her; there was nothing more she could say.

"Sara, if I break my contract in Ohio, they could sue me. At the least it would ruin my reputation."

"And after you finish the job in Ohio, what happens then?"

"There's no way I can know!"

He released her hand and stood to pace angrily down the side aisle while she sat in silent misery.

Forgetting her throbbing ankle, she went to him. She put her arms around him and clung to him. For longer than either realized, they stood locked together, her face pressed against the smooth wool of his overcoat, trying to forget the things that were ripping them apart.

"If I knew why you feel this way about moving, it might help me," he said forlornly, burying his face in her hair, the perfume of her shampoo released by the snow that had melted there.

Scenes from the past raced through her mind, but all of them seemed so trivial, taken separately: her mother crying because her father had to be away from them for six months; her brother furious because he had to leave his hockey team in midseason; Sara eating alone in a school cafeteria filled with people who knew each other, or walking down a dusty street, stung to the quick because a false new friend had called her a nasty name. No single thing she could tell him would explain how much she hated being the stranger, how much she feared inflicting this kind of life on herself and her children if she ever had any.

"I'm afraid . . ." she began.

"With me you can't be," he said desperately. "Sara, maybe you were shy when you were younger, but you've outgrown that. You can handle yourself in any situation. You showed me that today; I'm the one who acted like a jerk, coming on to you with twenty other people at the table."

"That wasn't too smooth," she said with the ghost of a smile playing over her features. "I was ready to jab you with my fork."

"You're a fighter. You can handle my way of life, thrive on it. You don't need to hide away in your snug cottage like a frigid old maid."

"Jason!"

"All right—like a retiring single person. That may sound better, but it amounts to the same thing. Dropping out of the mainstream of life."

She walked away from him and hid her face against the cold glass of a window, watching her breath cloud it.

"Sara!"

She responded to the agony in his voice, rising as it did to the high ceiling of the church. The massive wooden beams, traditionally shaped like the skeleton of a ship, seemed to absorb his words, leaving naked pain between them.

He pressed his mouth against hers, holding them together without pressure, their hands and bodies not touching. It was a chaste meeting of their lips, not a kiss, but Sara felt molten lead pour through her body, searing her soul with longing for this man.

After turning away from her, he walked toward the

altar but didn't see it, bunching his shoulders against her rejection like a man about to be scourged.

"Where do we go from here?" he asked in a stricken voice.

"I don't know," she whispered, forcing him to turn back to her to hear her words.

"It can't go on the way it has been. There is a limit to how much torture I can stand."

"Jason, I don't want you to suffer!"

"I know, darling. I know."

He came to her, letting her rest against him, shuddering when her hand lightly touched his cheek, but not responding.

"The snow has nearly stopped. I guess we won't have another blizzard," he said.

Had she been hoping for one, hoping Jason would be stranded with her again, hoping the elements would help her keep him with her?

"I'll walk back to your aunt's house now. Give me your keys, and I'll bring your car here. Then you won't have to worry about getting it home. You'd better put ice on your ankle and keep it elevated as soon as you get home. Go to the doctor if it bothers you."

"Yes."

Minutes seemed like hours as she waited for Jason to return, the peace of the church becoming oppressive as she desperately groped for a solution to their dilemma.

There wasn't one.

The door flew inward, startling her, even though she'd been anticipating his return.

"Let me help you down the steps. They're slippery," he said.

Outside the church, the door secured behind them, he picked her up and carried her to level ground, his face impersonal and remote in spite of their physical closeness. She was losing him; she could sense it as surely as she could feel the bitterly cold air hitting her face. She knew the words that would bring him back, but fear and confusion kept them locked inside her.

Jason helped her to the front door of her house, his eyes dull and hurt as they bored into hers.

"I don't know where we go from here," he said.

"Do you want to come in . . . to talk?"

"Is there anything else to say, Sara?"

He was challenging the last remnants of her pride, forcing her to answer him coldly and sternly. "No, I think we've said everything."

He left her standing in the cold, turning from her without a backward glance. She watched him walk back for his car until tears obscured her vision, blurring her eyes and scorching her heart.

Days passed, stretching into weeks. Sara put her calendar in a drawer and muted the sound on her phone, threw herself into her work at the bank, made and bought Christmas gifts for her relatives and friends, baked enough cookies to provide coffee break treats at the bank for months, shopped, wrapped, and created new decorations to use inside and outside her house, dipped into her spinning wheel money to keep herself frantically busy.

Winter came to stay, and she developed a cough that made her so tired and listless she finally went to the doctor for medication. The hacking cough subsided, but the shadows under her eyes grew darker, causing Rachel to cluck over her with genuine concern. Sara deeply appreciated her concern, but she became uncomfortable with her great-aunt's questions. When her parents succeeded, with great difficulty, in reaching her by phone, she knew Aunt Rachel had been telling tales in her letters. She laughed and joked with her father and reassured her mother that she missed them but was fine. She hoped they bought it.

Keeping her hands busy was the easy part; Jason preyed on her mind, in her dreams, at work, at home. Nothing she did pushed him out of her consciousness for long. The phone never rang without causing a panicky moment of hope; the doorbell made her heart stick in her throat, but her anticipation was all for nothing.

## CHAPTER NINE

"When your mother was a girl, she loved sugaring," Aunt
Rachel said, tying a sturdy yellow denim apron with red
piping around her gently rounded waist. "She was more
a little sister to me than a niece, you know. I never felt old
enough to be her aunt, and of course, my sister was much
older than I was."

Sara had volunteered her kitchen and her help in making maple sugar candy for her great-aunt's class, a Christmas tradition in the first grade from the days when Rachel
had been a novice teacher. Now, the Sunday before the
holiday, they were working together to produce large
molded Santas for each child.

"I should have brought you an apron, dear. This can be
a sticky job."

"Nothing can hurt these old jeans," Sara said, teasing
her aunt just a little because the older woman firmly be-
lieved that blue denim pants were for farmers and little
boys, not young ladies.

The dark amber syrup sat in a gallon jug on the kitchen
table, hoarded away by Rachel for her annual Christmas
candy. Uncapping it, Sara drank in the aroma, almost

tasting the maple sweetness, unlike any other flavor in existence.

"My uncle Elmer used to drag tanks of maple syrup through the snow with a team of horses," Rachel said wistfully. "Maple sugar wasn't always a luxury, you know. A hundred years ago farmers sold it in bulk just as cheaply as white sugar. People used it in their coffee, in recipes, on fruit. Of course, then the highest-quality maple sugar had the least flavor, just the opposite of today."

The rubber Santa molds, used for thousands of Christmas treats in the past, lay beside the raw syrup, and Sara wondered how long it would take to fill them enough times for the whole first grade. Not that it really mattered. Time hung so heavily on her hands she'd be glad to help her aunt all night if necessary.

"Now watch me, dear, and we'll get a couple of pans going at once."

Rachel poured about a half inch of syrup in a stainless steel pan, rapidly bringing it to a boil as she stirred with a wooden spoon. The dark liquid bubbled furiously, threatening to rise over the edge of the pan. After nearly ten minutes of steamy cooking, a test drop formed a ball in a cup of cold water, and Rachel immersed the kettle to its brim in cold water.

"Things go fast now," the older woman warned, stirring the syrup energetically for a few minutes until it looked like sticky brown taffy.

"Now we rush," she explained, reheating the gooey mass, which turned to liquid again in a very brief time.

"I understand the process up to now," Sara said, "but why reheat it?"

"Oh, that's the important step in getting a good texture. Just watch."

In another half minute Rachel was pouring the crystallized liquid into molds. Sara watched in fascination as the sugar Santas began to cool to a mouth-watering tan, perfect maple sugar treats for Christmas.

"No need to wash the pot between batches," her aunt said. "The little bit stuck to the pan acts as a starter."

The two women labored side by side, enjoying the steamy sweetness that filled the air. Overheated, Sara had to keep blotting her face with a paper towel, wondering if they'd ever have enough sugar Santas to fill her great-aunt's gift-giving needs. As they worked, Rachel's list seemed to lengthen, until it was obvious that everyone from the newspaper carrier to the school principal's grandchildren would receive maple candy. By the time they finished the little tan figures were covering every imaginable surface in her kitchen, plus the waxed-paper surface of her card table in the living room.

"I thought, if you don't mind, dear," Rachel said when the cooking utensils and molds had been washed, "I'll run up to the hospital to see Jimmy Harper's mother, then come back this evening to help you wrap these."

"You'll do no such thing! I'll wrap them, and you can pick them up on your way to school tomorrow."

"Would you mind, Sara? It would be such a big help. I haven't quite finished the sweater I'm knitting for Maida, and I promised I'd look in on the Willards for a glass of wine tonight. Their son sent a case from California for Christmas."

"Enjoy yourself," Sara said, brushing her aunt's cheek with an affectionate kiss. "I haven't a thing to do tonight."

It was true. Sara filled her time with every conceivable activity from attending a town meeting to substituting on a bowling team, but empty hours haunted her. Sometimes, in the company of others, she could momentarily forget about Jason, the hollow feeling in her chest subsiding for a while. Alone, the pain returned as she remembered how wonderful it felt to be in his arms. The familiar yearning tightness made her ache for him, but her mind deplored her weakness. Everything was finished between them; something that should never have begun was now part of the past. She'd gotten over Bill, and she would do the same with Jason.

Visions of a warm, bubbly bath were making her hurry through some kitchen-cleaning chores when the phone ran in her bedroom. The sound was still muted, but she seemed to hear it no matter where she was in the house. She walked slowly to answer it, not at all excited about the prospect of talking to Roger. He'd been gone for more than a week at a banking seminar, and undoubtedly he was checking in to tell her he was back. Hearing a blow-by-blow account of every meeting he'd attended wasn't for her tonight. She'd beg off on the excuse that she had to wrap an army of maple Santas.

"Sara?"

The voice on the other end of the line took her breath away. She'd given up hope of ever hearing from Jason again, her reason telling her that this was best. His Christmas departure time was only days away.

"Sara, I'd like to see you," he said matter-of-factly, sounding as if things were perfectly normal between them.

"I don't know."

"I'm not giving you a choice," he said grimly. "I'm calling from the pay phone outside the gas station. I'll be there in three minutes."

"Why did you bother to call?"

"A courtesy," he said dryly. "Also, I want you to know that if you don't let me in, I'll see you at the bank tomorrow. I think right now would be better, don't you?"

"You never will take no for an answer."

"I've had to swallow a lot of no answers from you."

The phone went dead in her ear, and she caught a glimpse of her face in the dresser mirror. Her cheeks were still flushed from the heat of candy cooking, and her long hair, usually bouncy with end curls, looked lank from the steam. She brushed it quickly and tied it into a ponytail on the top of her head, not caring that the style was better suited to a fifteen-year-old. After hastily sprinkling cold

159

water on her face to revive herself, she gave up trying to improve her appearance. She smelled like maple sugar, a few stray splashes were sticking darkly to the front of her short-sleeved red T-shirt, and her hair was bobbing around like a horse's tail. She was a mess, but it really didn't matter how she looked for Jason.

Her doorbell pealed out with three impatient blasts, but she moved slowly, hating the trembling feeling in her legs and the dampness of her palms. She didn't even have a photograph of Jason, but he was so vividly etched on her brain that she visualized him perfectly, seeing the little things that set him off: the faint pinpoint of a mole on his left earlobe; the few blackish brown hairs that stood out on the crown of his head regardless of how carefully he combed them into place; the way his hands unconsciously balled into fists when he was angry. His impatience seemed to radiate through the door, and although she felt like a coward, she was afraid to open it.

As if sensing her reluctance, he rang again, using the mechanical sound to insist on being admitted.

"I thought you weren't going to answer," he said with a humorless smile when she did open the door.

"You'd probably just force the lock with a credit card."

"You still haven't called a locksmith." It was a rebuke.

"You didn't succeed in making me afraid in my own town."

"That was never my intention. I just think women living alone should take reasonable precautions against break-ins."

"Are you here to check on my security arrangements?"

"Of course not. This place smells like maple syrup."

"Aunt Rachel and I have been making sugar Santas for her class."

"Is she still here?" His eyes narrowed.

"No. Would it matter?"

"I guess not. Are you going to take my coat?"

"I don't think you'll be here that long."

160

"Is that what you hope?"

"Yes," she said, lying.

He moved closer and caught her girlish ponytail in one finger.

"Cute. That maple smell is making me feel like a kid again. Are there any pots to lick?"

"They're all washed, but we do have a few broken Santas for sampling."

"And maybe some coffee?"

"Jason, why are you here?"

"You should take lessons on being a good hostess from your aunt Rachel."

"All right, I'll make coffee," she agreed testily, "but, Jason, I can't go through the whole thing again. I'm cured. There's nothing else to be said."

"You're a lousy liar," he said, staring at her with hard, uncompromising eyes.

Afraid that he'd touch her, she hurried into the kitchen, where she measured grounds into the automatic coffee-maker with unsteady hands. She lost count of the scoops and decided it served him right if the coffee was so strong it made his hair stand on end.

He was examining the Santas with exaggerated interest. Finally he selected a piece of broken foot and sucked on it thoughtfully.

"Not bad. Very good, in fact. I've never tasted maple sugar made in a kitchen at home. Rich but delicious."

His charade was getting on her nerves, but she tried to remain cool, setting out mugs and filling them when the coffee was ready.

"We'll have to go into the living room," she said, gesturing at the table crowded with candy. "I still have to wrap all these Santas tonight."

When she was seated across the room from him, she asked, "How is the house coming?," really wanting to know how soon he'd disappear from her life forever.

"I'm finished."

161

He sipped the steaming beverage without taking his eyes from her.

"You're probably excited about your next job then."

"I'm too tired to be excited," he said, the weariness showing in the drawn look around his eyes. "I'm not used to working sixteen hours a day and still having insomnia."

She stayed silent, sensing that his nights were tormented by longings, as hers were.

"The house in Ohio is a huge late Victorian mansion," he said dryly. "The last owner willed it to the city with a trust fund to restore it and convert it into a combination community center and museum. There are eleven fireplaces, seven of them solid oak and all but one defaced with layers of paint. Pink paint in one bedroom."

There wasn't any of his usual enthusiasm in his voice, but he continued the recitation.

"A curving stairway dominates the front of the house. I imagine a lot of couples will want to use it for weddings when it's open to the public. Just the thing for a bride to descend with a long train."

"It sounds like a very nice house," Sara said, more depressed than interested.

"It is. The original builder tried to make it resemble a castle, complete with turrets and a large tower. The outside has been well maintained; but it was rented several times to fly-by-night businesses, and the interior alterations are ugly. It will take six months just to rip out all the so-called improvements."

Once his work had seemed like a safe, neutral topic. Now it hurt unbearably to imagine him working alone in some monster of a house so far away from her.

"Of course, it's not all bad. There's a fantastic dumbwaiter, and all the original marble bathroom fixtures are there. The lady of the house could summon her servants through a speaking tube, and rows of built-in racks by the furnace served as an early-day clothes dryer. You'd have to see it to believe how clever some of the features are."

162

"I imagine it took a flock of underpaid lackeys to keep the master's household in order."

"Now you're the one seeing things as they really were," he said with a sad smile. "That's a switch."

"Why did you come here, Jason?"

"To see you."

She shook her head dolefully. "It only opens the wounds."

"Mine haven't healed."

"But nothing's changed."

"No, but this self-denial game we're playing is idiotic. People always want things more when they can't have them."

"That's why you came here, to 'have' me? To get me out of your system?"

"You make it sound like all I need is a simple cathartic," he said, rising to his feet and looking bitterly down at her.

He walked to the window and stared out at the street with his hands thrust deeply into his pockets.

"There's been enough snow for good skiing," he said hesitantly.

She was standing, too, but keeping her distance, knowing what might happen if she drew too near.

"I'm going to ask you something," he said, turning to face her, "but I want you to promise not to give me your answer now."

"I don't understand."

"Just promise me you won't say yes or no right now."

"All right. I promise."

Her stomach was churning nervously, and she was sure his question would cause more uncertainty and anxiety.

"I have reservations for ten days at a ski lodge. That will be my Christmas, New Year's holiday break. I want you to come with me, no strings attached. When the vacation is over, I won't pressure you to leave with me. We can enjoy the little time we have together and part friends."

"You said you didn't want to be my friend."

"I want to be your lover, if not forever, at least for enough time to get rid of the worst ache I've ever felt."

"Will ten days do that?"

"No, damn it," he snapped, taking her shoulders in a painfully hard grasp, "but I'm the practical one, remember. If I can't have all that I want, I'll settle for a few crumbs."

"I don't know if—"

"No, you promised. No answer now. I'll come here tomorrow evening. Give me your answer then. I'll be packed and on my way. If you're going, be ready to leave. If not, well, I guess it will be good-bye."

"My job—I don't know if I can get time off."

"For God's sake, don't give me excuses, Sara. Be honest enough to say yes or no because that's the way you want it. Either way I can't fight it anymore. Here." He tossed a brightly colored pamphlet on a chair. "A brochure from the lodge. It shows where it is and what there is to do there. I have room one forty-eight reserved, a balcony room overlooking one of the ruins."

Looking into her face, he saw agony and indecision and groaned in frustration.

"We'd have a good time, the best," he said persuasively.

"I don't doubt it," she said, turning her back and sounding faraway.

"Look at me," he ordered.

Obeying only because her eyes were so hungry for the sight of him, she met his gaze for an instant, then lowered her head.

One hand tentatively touched her shoulder, ran down the length of her arm, and took her hand in his.

"Before you decide," he said, "remember how it can be with us. I don't believe you can turn your back on what we've shared."

His arms encircled her, drawing her closer, and his lips touched hers. As though this lightest of contacts had ignit-

164

ed a brush fire in his emotions, he crushed her against his length, smashing his mouth against hers with an intensity that sent her reeling.

"You see why I'm willing to settle for anything I can get," he said savagely, and then he was gone, leaving her house in a tomblike silence, broken only by her quiet weeping.

Locked in his arms, she would have done anything for him. She wanted to rip off her clothes and beg him to take her right there, willing to prostrate herself at his feet to quench the fire coursing through her. Not even in the heat of his lovemaking had she ever felt so out of control, so wanton. Shaking like a palsy victim, she knew that Jason had a terrible power over her, and it frightened her to the very core.

Cried out but still sunk in misery, she finally dragged herself to the bathroom, where she filled the tub and scrubbed every inch of her body with punishing harshness. She finally fell onto her bed in a stupor.

Jason had turned her into a creature of blind desires, a woman without a will of her own. There was a weakness in her that made her lose all sense of purpose, all thought for the future, when she was under his spell. Her love for him was like a poison, turning her well-ordered life into a shambles.

The healing relief of sleep wasn't for her. Her mattress was no more restful than a bed of coals, and she paced through the house restlessly. At last she remembered her promise to wrap the army of sugar Santas lying all over her kitchen. With fingers made clumsy by her agitation, she began wrapping the maple figures in plastic wrap, securing each one on the back with a bit of cellophane tape and piling them carefully in boxes between layers of crumpled wax paper. Working with robotlike indifference, she managed to finish the job with only a few casualties and tossed the broken pieces into her cookie jar for lack of a better place.

Before she finally fell into bed to toss restlessly for more hours than she cared to count, she knew that going on a skiing trip with Jason was out of the question. If she went with him, she'd never leave him. Facing her own weakness was devastating, but she knew how vulnerable she was. If she let him get close again, she would become his camp follower, his woman, regardless of whether or not she wore a wedding ring. The home, the family she craved would be forgotten forever, while the two of them wandered across the country at his whim, hardly unpacking before they packed again. Her only salvation was to stay away from him.

Finally, when her decision was so firm that nothing could shake it, she dropped into a dream-plagued sleep.

Monday lasted a hundred hours, or so it seemed to Sara, manning her cage at the bank but scarcely able to count to ten. She shortchanged one rather irritable man and gave too much money to another, fortunately honest person. She tried to cover her mistakes with apologies but eventually attracted Roger's attention.

"You're not off your feed again, are you?" he asked her. "It's not like you to make errors."

"Just the rush of Christmas," she alibied weakly. "I'm really sorry, Roger."

"Well, if you're sure you're not sick again."

He was distracted by a fellow Rotarian approaching his desk, but Sara could feel his eyes checking on her for the rest of the day. Was he worried about her, or was he afraid she'd give away bank money? Either way, his concern was irritating; it was her responsibility if she was short at the end of the day. Annoyance with Roger did help her concentrate on her job, but Jason's invitation was never far from her thoughts. Deciding not to go should have ended it, but the finality of her decision hurt unbearably.

Once, in midafternoon, she was sure she couldn't let him go without spending these last precious days with him. She imagined what it would be like to stay ten full

166

days and nights with him, being together in the best sense of the word, loving, playing, loving again.

But would they really be together? As long as he was planning to go his way and she was staying behind, there could never be a meaningful bonding. Without commitment they would only be having an affair, unsatisfying, fraught with tension and misunderstandings. Jason hadn't convinced her when he said there would be no strings; he was making a promise that neither of them was capable of keeping. Because they felt the way they did, the longing for permanence, for dominance would destroy their happiness and make a farce of his intentions.

Be honest, she told herself angrily. You won't go with Jason because you're too weak to refuse him when you're in his arms.

Jason had said he'd come in the evening. Why hadn't he been more specific about time? She bought some groceries she didn't need, returned a book to the library, even though it wasn't due and she hadn't read it, and filled the half-full tank of her car with gas. Stopping at Aunt Rachel's, she visited as long as her conscience would allow, knowing her great-aunt had to attend a Christmas program at school that evening.

The sky wasn't as black as her mood when she finally went home, and she didn't know how she'd stand it if she had to wait long for her confrontation with Jason.

When she did hear his car pull into the driveway, she knew he'd come too early. She wasn't emotionally prepared for the scene that was sure to follow her refusal to go.

Then he was there, filling her entryway with a stance that challenged her even before he said a word.

"Are you going to tell me or make me ask?" His voice was cold and reserved.

"I want to go, but . . . Jason, I can't have an affair with you."

"An affair?" He laughed scornfully. "I've asked you to

167

live with me, marry me, spend the rest of your life with me. Why are you making it sound like I'm propositioning you?"

"I didn't mean to, but ten days would only torture us both."

"It's an open-ended invitation. Ten days. Ten years. Ten lifetimes. Take your choice."

"I'm not going," she said, the words nearly strangling her.

"Then there's only one thing to say, isn't there? Goodbye, Sara."

He closed the door behind him.

Her misery had passed the point where tears would help as she sank down on the couch in her empty house. He was gone, really gone. Now she had to patch her life back together, and she didn't have the energy to begin.

The night before Christmas Eve Roger asked her to have dinner with him. More out of habit than from any desire to go, she agreed, wondering for the first time whether Roger or any other man would be part of her future. Some of Rachel's single friends had never had an opportunity to form lasting relationships with men; a very few, her great-aunt in particular, seemed to have admirers and gentlemen friends but no interest in pair bonding. Was Sara also destined to live alone, never making a commitment to share her life, remaining single, unencumbered but uncherished, always surrounded by friends, not by loved ones?

After the emotional upheaval of loving Jason, single life looked appealing. Having loved so deeply with such great pain, she didn't feel that she'd ever be ready to risk her affections again. Jason would call her an old maid; militant feminists would admire her as an independent woman. Her aunt most likely would find another eligible bachelor and try her matchmaking talents again, undaunted by the fact that nothing had developed with Jason

Marsh. None of this mattered; Sara's survival was what counted, and for the moment she found the thought of even a casual relationship with another man too depressing to consider.

Had Jason been right in saying that if Roger hadn't existed, she would have dreamed him up? The young banker was respectable, loyal to his family, kind, intelligent, nice-looking, pleasant, and a bloody bore, she realized with a jolt. She'd cast him in a role, and he'd played the part admirably well, but where was the passion, the love that could exist between two people? There would never be any deep feelings between Roger and her, and she was playing an unfair game with him, knowing as she did that having a family of his own was beginning to appeal to him.

She dressed in the conservative style Roger liked, her forest green suit with a buff jersey blouse, and pulled her hair back into a bun, a severe style that made her features look sharper but not unattractive.

Driving farther than was prudent in the uncertain weather, Roger seemed determined to make a big evening of it, something he rarely did on a weeknight. He ordered a bottle of wine chilled in a bucket of ice before dinner at The Rodundo, a fashionable steak house, then insisted that they try the tenderloin-lobster tail combination. Remembering Jason devouring a lobster, his face darkly handsome over a wide paper bib that made most men look ridiculous, she enjoyed her meal not at all. Roger was so full of commentaries on his seminar that she wasn't called upon to keep up much of a conversation, but the dinner dragged on.

A small combo played old-fashioned big-band music, and Roger invited her to dance, not his favorite activity but one she usually loved. Remembering how it felt to be in Jason's arms, she declined, unable to bear having any other man touch her.

The evening wasn't a great success.

Anticipating Roger's usual trio of kisses, Sara swiftly opened the door as soon as his car came to a stop in her driveway.

"Wait, Sara, please." His voice sounded unnaturally tense.

Closing the door again with misgivings, she looked at him with dull eyes, knowing it was unfair to hate him because he wasn't Jason, but suddenly feeling very, very tired of Roger.

"We haven't known each other very long, Sara," he said in his firm, speech-making voice, "but you must know I've grown fond of you. I'd like you to be my wife."

"Fond, Roger? You're asking me to marry you on the basis of fondness?" She unintentionally raised her voice, startled as she was by his abrupt proposal.

"Sara, we've been close. I thought we'd be a good father and mother team."

"You'd be a wonderful father, Roger; you care so much for your niece and nephew. But doesn't a marriage have to have more than that going for it? Love, desire?"

"Well, of course," he stammered.

"Oh, Roger." She touched his hand, groping for a way to be kind in her refusal. He'd been her friend, and for that she was grateful.

"You don't love me, and I don't love you," she said. "We'd both be settling for second best."

"Who told you about Nana?" he asked, sounding stricken.

"Nana? I've never heard of a Nana."

"Just past history," he said uncomfortably. "Under-graduate stuff that didn't work out. I thought maybe you'd heard gossip. You know how small towns are. Make a mountain out of a molehill."

"Roger, I don't think we should see each other any-more," she said wearily, not wanting to hear anything at all about his lost romance.

"I didn't expect my marriage proposal to offend you so

much you'd refuse to see me again," he said, coming back to his purpose for their evening together.

"Oh, no, don't think that, please don't. Any woman would be pleased and flattered to have you ask, Roger. I just don't think we're meant for each other. We're too different. It would be too much a marriage of convenience. I hope this doesn't mean we can't remain friends."

"I guess not," he said dubiously.

She leaned forward, kissed him swiftly on the cheek, thanked him, and left him.

Sara's conscience compelled her to report for work as usual at the bank the next morning, but she couldn't look forward to the combination of tension and tedium that faced her. Her analytical powers, sharpened by misery, warned her that Roger wasn't going to be a good loser, and in spite of his mild exterior, his ego demanded success. His failure with her wasn't going to sit well with him.

Her only consolation was that the next day was a bank holiday, Christmas Day. Roger nodded curtly when she went to her drawer to prepare for the day's business, and for the rest of the morning he pointedly ignored her. The afternoon was worse; he reprimanded her in front of a customer for an error that wasn't her fault. In spite of her determination to treat him with deference and courtesy, she clearly saw that his feelings had been hurt. Was he so blind that he couldn't see they never could have had a successful marriage? How much punishment would he have to mete out to avenge his wounded pride?

To her relief, she discovered that she really didn't care. Roger's petty jabs passed over her because she didn't feel guilty for refusing his proposal. Such an abrupt business-like offer wouldn't have tempted her even if Jason hadn't existed.

The day after Christmas she was going to map out a campaign to find work better suited to her training and inclination. A rumor was circulating that Sibley's Tavern was changing ownership, and this was just the kind of restaurant that might have need of her skills. A family ran it now, but the new owner might be in need of management help. In the meantime, she wouldn't let herself be bothered by Roger's snubs and barbs. Maybe every woman had to have one Roger in her life; Sara had met him too late to settle for the security he offered. Since knowing Jason, she was incapable of accepting a passionless relationship.

Christmas Eve in Banbury was a warm, companionable time; village young people serenaded from house to house, their sweet voices singing familiar carols, as a light snow made the streets and rooftops glisten. Sara opened her house to carolers and friends, ladling spicy hot mulled cider into her grandmother's punch cups, until it was time for the traditional midnight service.

Walking across town with a group of neighbors, carried along by the enthusiasm of their children, she felt a part of something larger than herself. The spirit of the season brought her a brief respite from the pain of being apart from Jason, and the creche scene under a towering pine tree inside the church reminded her of the happy Christmas Eves spent with her family around trees laden with colored lights, glass bulbs, and homemade decorations.

Much to her surprise, her phone rang just after she returned home, bringing her back to the bleak reality of missing Jason. Her hand trembled when she lifted the receiver, so sure was she that Jason couldn't just disappear from her life forever.

"Sarie, Merry Christmas," a man's voice said, sounding faraway and warmly familiar.

"Dave!"

"And family."

"It's so good to hear your voice."

"We're all here waiting to wish you happy holidays," her brother said. "Jan and Nichole, who just lost a front tooth, can you believe that? And Todd. Todd doesn't have much to say yet, but we sure hear from him all day long."

"I'm so glad you called. You've timed it perfectly, I just got back from midnight service."

For brief minutes she was part of their circle, loving them all so much she wanted to cry.

"When are you coming to see us?" her brother asked before he said good-bye.

"Oh, Dave, not soon. I can't afford long vacations."

"I'm not talking about a vacation. Come live with us for a while. You'd love the Islands."

"Thank you, but no, Dave. I'm a permanent resident of Vermont now," she assured him.

"I'll believe that twenty years from now. All us Gilmans have gypsy blood."

"Not this one, Dave, not this one," she said sadly, feeling the warmth of his family's call slipping away from her.

"Sara," Jan said, taking the phone from her husband, "that invitation comes from all of us. Nichole would love to see Aunt Sarie, and you and I could have a ball."

Before Sara could answer, her sister-in-law broke off, torn from the phone by an urgent squeal from her young son.

"Would you come stay with us?" Nichole said in her little-girl coaxing voice, then saying good-bye at her father's direction before Sara was forced to give a negative answer.

"Women, you give them a phone, and they bankrupt you with the bill," he said jokingly. "At least keep us in mind, Sarie. We miss you."

"I miss all of you. Thanks for calling, Dave. It really was good talking to you."

"As if I wouldn't wish my little sister a Merry Christmas! Bye now, love."

"Good-bye, Dave," she said, then heard the phone go

dead in her hand. The broken connection seemed to sever more than a conversation.

After her brother's call the house seemed colder and very, very empty. She washed punch cups and straightened the living room, putting the gifts she'd be distributing the next day on the coffee table, congratulating herself on how well she was managing to keep busy. Maybe she'd weather this storm in good shape after all; no one went through her whole life moaning over an impossible love.

When at last she crawled under her comforter, she couldn't seem to get warm. The thought of getting an electric blanket or heating pad occurred to her, but she knew neither was a solution. Even as she dozed off, her arm reached out for a man who wasn't there.

## CHAPTER TEN

Fewer people gathered at Aunt Rachel's for Christmas than for Thanksgiving, but all the celebrants were familiar, their faces remembered from the November feast. The Willards, Colonel Barnham, Maida, and several other friends arrived before Sara, filling the space under the tinsel-draped tree with brightly wrapped packages.

Sara added her gifts to the pile: a furry robe for her great-aunt, an antique corkscrew for the Willards' collection, a tray of imported cheeses for the colonel, and books for the others. Exclaiming over her presents as she opened those given to her, she tried to throw herself, body and spirit, into the cordial gathering of friends, but the consciousness that something was missing nagged at her.

"I love it, Aunt Rachel," she said, hugging her surprised relative vigorously after opening up her gift, a striking burgundy ski sweater with a stylized pattern worked in white, praying that her aunt wouldn't see how choked up she was, not because of the present but because it was Jason's favorite color and he'd never see it.

Not unexpectedly Mr. Willard gave bottles of fine wine as gifts, and his quiet white-haired wife had crocheted thick, practical potholders for everyone. Books, knickknacks, fruitcakes, and clothing accessories changed hands with appreciative comments, but Sara felt remote, present with the group but not sharing their enjoyment. She forced herself to sound happy but couldn't shake the feeling that she was an onlooker. It wasn't just that she was younger than the others; she couldn't seem to return the love that flowed her way. Her emotions had turned to ashes, blistered on the fire ignited by Jason, seared by their parting.

Playing the part expected of her, she talked a little too fast, thanked the gift givers a little too enthusiastically, and worked hard at being her aunt's cohostess, running back and forth to the kitchen, checking on the succulent crown roast baking in the oven, even though it didn't need attention.

Again the colonel carved at the table, and Sara realized that her own mood had escaped her great-aunt's notice because she was preoccupied with her gentleman friend. Aunt Rachel's other guests as well were too intrigued by the budding romance between the pair to wonder at Sara's agitated mood. She smiled in relief when she realized this, becoming more quiet, but the afternoon passed with the slowness of a parade of turtles.

The first to leave, Sara hugged them all, grateful that they'd included her in their circle, even though she hadn't been cheered by the day's festivities. The day would have been painfully empty without them, but gratitude was all she felt. Because of Jason, she was alone in a crowd, a stranger in their midst. He'd done this to her, shattered her illusion that she belonged.

With her arms piled high with gifts and leftovers that Rachel insisted she take, she nearly missed seeing the hastily scrawled note laying between her storm door and the inner door. It was from her neighbors, asking that she call their house immediately. Unable to imagine why either the middle-aged Reeses or their two high-school-aged sons would want to contact her, she slowly deposited her load on the kitchen table and hung up her coat, rather reluctant to talk to anyone else that day.

The worry that something might be wrong finally prodded her to phone; after all, her neighbors might have a serious emergency and need her to watch their house or look after their poodle.

"Mr. Reese, this is Sara Gilman. I found your note."

"Oh, you caught me just in time before we drive out in the country to see my wife's folks. Tom and I will be right over."

He hung up without giving her a chance to ask why, so all she could do was wait for them. When the front doorbell rang, she was rather surprised; the Reeses were back-door people. They would have a special reason for coming to the front.

"Hello" died on her lips when she saw her neighbor and his red-haired son standing outside with a large antique spinning wheel.

"Fellow brought this to our house 'cause you weren't home," Mr. Reese said, as pleased as if the gift had come from him. "Left me this card to hand to you. Where do you want us to put it?"

"I don't know . . . I didn't expect . . . well, I guess here by the window."

She watched, dumbfounded, while the man and his son carefully positioned the spinning wheel in the spot she'd indicated. It was a large piece, filling the bay window area and protruding into the room.

"I can't thank you enough," she said.

"Don't thank us. Thank the fellow's giving it to you. Here, now, take the card. And Merry Christmas!"

Running one trembling hand over the smooth wood, she knew she wasn't mistaken. This was the spinning wheel she had lost to Jason, the lovely antique that had brought them together. But Jason had bought it for his client; he'd never intended to keep it himself.

So moved she could hardly open the envelope, she

managed to draw out a sheet of Jason's business stationery and read the words written with felt pen in large, bold strokes.

Sara, my love—
I'll always see you beside this—spinning dreams.
Jason

Her eyes were so full of tears she could hardly see, and she pressed the note against her breast, hardly daring to believe what he had done. Pain rose in a wave, engulfing her until she cried out his name aloud, loving him so much it was tearing her apart.

Down on her knees beside the spinning wheel, she ran her fingers over the surface, needing to touch something Jason had touched, desperately reassuring herself that it was real. For a long while she stayed that way, finally becoming aware of her own sobs, the only sound to break the heavy silence in her house.

"I'm a fool," she said aloud, reaching the absolute depths of regret. "There's nothing in life I want more than him."

She stood stiffly in her cozy living room, seeing it for the first time as an empty room in a lifeless house. As often as her parents had moved, their home had never seemed barren; the love they shared as a family had filled it with something far more important than furniture and other possessions. Without the love of special people, life was only a hollow shell; without Jason, her life was a charade, an illusion.

She suffered because she missed all of them, her parents, her brother and his family, but especially Jason. That she could have let him go, knowing that he deeply loved her, was a burden she would bear for the rest of her life. How could she ever think that places mattered more than love?

Slowly she walked to the couch and picked up her worn

pillow, remembering the hours of pleasure she'd had working the words: "Home is where the heart is." The needle in her fingers had outlined the letters in wool, but she'd never understood the message. Her heart was with Jason; nothing else mattered anymore.

How low should she set the temperature reading on the thermostat? Focusing on practical details helped her pull herself together and plan rationally. She was going to Jason, not tomorrow but immediately. This meant leaving her house unoccupied; should she ask someone to watch it?

How long would she be gone? That was the question that had to be answered before she considered the house, and she just didn't know. Was the spinning wheel a goodbye gift? Had Jason given up on her, rejecting her because she had first rejected him? Or had he given it to her as a way of saying he wouldn't forget her? His note made her hope that this was the reason, but even then, did he still want her with him forever?

She was thinking of her house when all that mattered was Jason! With desperate haste she brought out her largest suitcase and threw in something from every drawer in her dresser, then dumped essential toiletries and cosmetics into her makeup bag. Her red dress, some skirts and slacks, a careless selection of blouses flew into her suitcase. She clicked shut the catches before she remembered her new ski sweater. And her shawl. She must take the paisley. She carried her luggage to the car, locked it in the trunk, and returned to gather the odds and ends that hadn't fitted: her nylon jacket, her purse, her wool scarf, the brochure from the ski lodge.

Even though she knew it wouldn't be the last time she ever saw her house, she said good-bye to it: the kitchen papered with yellow pineapples by a previous owner; the living room with its warm maple furniture; her bedroom with walls her favorite shade of pale eggshell blue. As an afterthought she turned down the furnace to fifty-five degrees; an unemployed bank teller couldn't afford to pile up huge heating bills. This done, she decided her house could take care of itself; it was only a collection of rooms, a place where she'd been hiding from the risks of love.

The streets were nearly deserted, the sleepy little village recouping from the holiday merriment. A pair of children in red and blue snowsuits were playing with a fuzzy new puppy on the snow-covered village green, but Sara barely noticed. The spell was broken; Banbury was no longer her haven. Belonging to one person was more exciting than walking on ground where her ancestors had lived, more vital to life than an attic full of memories, more comforting than knowing every face that passed on the street.

The roads were unfamiliar, and the early dusk was overtaking her; but she relied on the map in the brochure to find her way. Once she reached a main highway, she felt surer of reaching her destination without making any wrong turns. The trip might take several hours, driving as slowly as she was, but there was nothing to hold her up. Her gas tank was nearly full, and she wouldn't need to eat for a week after Aunt Rachel's dinner.

Light snow fell when she was half an hour from Banbury, but she drove out of the flurries in a few minutes. A heavy wind battered her car, but fortunately she was traveling on ice-free highways. The farther she went, the more unreal her life in Banbury seemed. Nothing existed but the car, the road, and Jason.

The ski lodge, well lit inside and out, was a large rustic building, the wood siding weathered to pewter gray. The parking lot indicated that business was good, the holiday break bringing skiers from a number of states, but Jason's car wasn't immediately visible among the many cars and vans, adding the worry that he might have changed his mind about going there to the gnawing anxiety she already felt. She could only pray that it was parked in the rear or hidden out of sight between two larger vehicles.

Now, when she was faced with the prospect of walking

in unexpected, all kinds of complications occurred to her. Should she take her suitcase and go to the registration desk? If she carried her case, she obviously should check in, but Jason had mentioned his room number, 148. She could go directly to it, leaving her suitcase in the car until she was sure of her welcome.

The awful possibility that Jason might have found other companionship flashed through her mind; it was an idea too dreadful to consider.

"You idiot!" she said aloud, forcing herself to leave the shelter of her car, changing her mind about her luggage.

Lugging the heavy suitcase with lopsided haste, she walked through the lobby, past the roaring fireplace, beyond a crowd of people who seemed to be having a marvelous time, up a flight of broad stairs with burnt orange carpeting.

Finding the room was easier than knocking on the door. Dropping the suitcase beside her feet, she clutched and reclutched her fist. Finally she rapped lightly with her knuckles. So nervous by now that she was grinding her teeth, she knocked again.

The door swung inward, and she thought she'd pass out from holding her breath before Jason finally reacted to her.

"Sara, come in," he said softly.

He saw her suitcase and reached for it, his hand touching hers, then quickly retracted.

"I'll take it," he said, motioning her into the room and closing the door.

Two double beds made the floor space minimal. The stiff gold spread of one was littered with maps, the folded highway guides of the kind indispensable to travelers.

"You're planning your trip to Ohio?" she asked when the silence between them seemed to stretch on forever.

"No. Sara, why are you here?"

Looking into his eyes, she gave him an answer without words, her face telling him everything. In two steps she

181

was in his arms, her face tilted to receive a kiss that they shared with a sense of breathless wonder.

His hair was slightly damp, and he was wearing a bright yellow terry-cloth robe and beaded moccasins. He was obviously still drying out from the shower, and a hint of spicy soap clung to his skin as she pressed her nose against his cheek, loving the feel and scent of him.

"Let me take your coat," he said, slipping it off her shoulders and tossing it on a chair beyond the jumble of maps on the bed.

"You look wonderful," he said, running his hands down the back of the dusty-rose crepe dress she'd worn to Aunt Rachel's. "Did you wear this for me?"

"No," she admitted, hearing the zipper part down the length of her back. "I went to Aunt Rachel's for Christmas."

Holding her close, he massaged her shoulders, working out the knots left by her tense drive. Slowly he eased the dress off her shoulders, kissing the length of her arms, pressing soft kisses on the faint blue veins, making her shudder with longing.

"I have to talk to you," she said brokenly as his hands traveled down her sides, pushing her dress over her hips until it fell to the floor.

"I never gave up hope that you might come," he said hoarsely.

"Jason, it's important."

"This is important."

He kissed the knuckles of her hand and guided it to the opening of his robe. His skin was cool to her touch, the matted hair still sticking to his skin from the shower. He pulled his robe tie away impatiently, letting the garment fall open, and drew her to him. Locked together for a breathtaking moment, they communicated without words, their bodies sending messages that wouldn't be denied.

"The spinning wheel . . ."

"Later," he said, throwing aside the spread on the map-free bed and pulling her down beside him. "Let me love you now, Sara."

"Love me," she whispered, the two single words carrying the whole weight of her love, telling him all he was desperate to hear.

She pulled his face to hers, clung to him, caressed with her lips, surrendered wholly when his mouth took possession of hers.

He sent his robe sailing to the other bed and removed her remaining garments, his impatience making his hands awkward but not robbing them of gentleness. Wanting the sweetness of their passion to go on forever, she turned from him, delaying their lovemaking, and buried her face in the pillow to hide her smile of sheer happiness. Parting the hair at the back of her neck, he buried his face there and pressed his mouth against the sensitive nape, making her quiver with anticipation.

Massaging her shoulders with firm fingers, he made every pore feel alive, and when his lips trailed soft kisses over the tingling skin, it took all her self-control to keep from turning and clinging to him. Stroking the length of her spine, he worked magic on her senses, making her writhe on the sheet under his sensuous kneading. Unable to bear his persuasive touch another moment, she twisted around to face him, to wrap her arms around him with a strength she'd never used before.

His hands cupped her buttocks, grinding their bodies together, their mouths locked in a kiss that brutally exorcised all the hurt they had done to each other. Rolling in a mock struggle, they were greedy for love, too inflamed for subtleties.

Locked against the demanding hardness of his body, she felt part of herself slipping away forever, her girlhood restraints forgotten with incredible ease as she grasped what it meant to be his woman. All her trust flowed out to him even as she braced herself for the expected stab of pain that didn't come. Instead, their joining made her float on the wings of desire, her body, being, and life totally in his power. Surrender didn't enslave her but rather made her his equal, a full partner in the heights of pleasure. Their desire blazed out of control, their bodies rocking in a wild crescendo of sensation. Her awareness became razor-sharp as she reveled in the power of his need, the grace of his movements, the fiery warmth of his skin wherever their bodies met.

Clutching his slippery hips and arching her back, she felt swamped by her frenzied need to give and take the utmost pleasure.

"You're so wonderful," he murmured, "so fantastic . . ."

Gradually she began to hear his soft, crooning words, names of endearment that added spice to their love feast, and above her she saw the intent darkness of his eyes and the incredible beauty of his face. Not even his passionate hammering distracted her from the sweet penetration of his kiss, telling her as it did that he loved her deeply, fully, completely.

Sounds filled their world: his breath ragged, both hearts pounding, her moans building to a sharp outcry as he carried her with him into the explosion, her legs instinctively locking him to her in a lovers' knot. Limp but euphoric, they collapsed together, savoring the aftershocks with loving hands and lips.

Hovering over him, she wiped his brow with a strand of her long hair, kissing his closed lids, teasing him with the tip of her tongue, waiting for the trembling in her thighs to subside.

"Never torture me like that again," he begged.

"Is that what I was just doing?"

"No, not then, not now, but I can't stand to go through the agony of thinking I've lost you again. I'm afraid everything else in my life will seem pale in comparison to what I feel for you."

184

"We should have talked first," she said, falling back on the pillow beside him. "About the spinning wheel . . ."

"Don't talk about that now," he said, sitting up and slowly recovering, kissing her lightly for a long moment before speaking again. "Come look at these maps with me."

"Look at maps?"

Her puzzlement prodded her to cross naked to the other bed, where he was unfolding a large map, heedless of his own bare skin in the cool room. Kneeling beside him, resting her hand first on his back and then on his thigh because not touching him seemed like a kind of punishment, she watched as he folded and refolded the crinkly paper until the segment he wanted lay under their gaze.

"The black X's are areas with heavy concentrations of Colonial and Georgian homes," he said, pointing with one hand while his other captured hers and held it. "The circles are areas where a lot of robber barons of the nineteenth century built their pseudocastles and gingerbread mansions."

"Why are you telling me this?"

"Just look. Here and here, you can draw a circle around this area in Massachusetts and New York. If we lived right in the center, I could find enough work to keep me busy for fifty years. I might have to buy my own plane, and sometimes it would mean being home on weekends only, but I think we could hack it, darling."

"Jason, what are you saying?"

A cold, shaky feeling made her reach for his discarded robe and wrap it around her shoulders in stunned disbelief.

"I'm telling you we can make it work, Sara. I have to go to Ohio, but maybe I can subcontract enough of the work to get away in a year, eighteen months at the most. I'm putting my cabin and land in northern Michigan on the market. There's a long stretch of water frontage, so I should be able to sell it for a good price. Then I'm going to buy and renovate a place for us."

"A permanent home?"

Afraid to believe in something she wanted so badly, she hid her expression from him, letting her hair fall as a shield on the sides of her face, gazing at the map with unseeing eyes.

"A combination business and home are what I had in mind. An inn, maybe something like Sibley's Tavern. You can run it when I'm busy on a job. A dining room, maybe a dozen or so rooms, more or less, for vacationers. A lakeside site would be best."

"Jason, I can't believe it!"

The happiness on her face reached out to him, pulling him to her for a lingering caress, neither of them noticing that their lips were swollen and tender.

"It won't be as easy as I'm making it sound," he warned. "This kind of place will be hard to find and priced out of sight. But I think we can swing it. We'll have time to look while we're in Ohio, and—"

"Jason, it's the most wonderful idea I've ever heard, but I have to tell you . . . you wouldn't let me tell you before—"

"I was terrified you'd tell me something I didn't want to hear," he said, drawing her close to his side. "That you were staying only the weekend maybe."

"No, I tried to tell you I'm staying forever."

"Forever? And Banbury?"

"It's only a place. I was looking for something permanent, but it wasn't a town or a house. I learned that the hard way after you left. No strange new house was ever as empty as mine when I realized you were gone for good."

"Sara."

He pulled her on top of him, crushing the maps beneath him as he cradled her face on his shoulder, running his fingers through the light mass of hair spread out around her face.

"I love the spinning wheel," she said softly, "but how could you give it to me? I thought it went to the Attwater house."

"It was my ace of trumps," he said with a low, wicked laugh. "My wedding present or my last-ditch stand, depending on how things worked out."

"When did you decide to give it to me?"

"The day I bought it."

"I don't believe you!"

She sat up and looked at him incredulously.

"Not when I first bought it," he said, laughing and pinning her on top of a crackly map. "Maybe after you made that chowder last until it was ice-cold so you wouldn't have to look at me."

"You're teasing me."

"Not entirely. Remember, I went to New York on Monday, just two days later. While I was there, I looked up an old friend who deals in antiques and told him the kind of spinning wheel I had to have for the Attwater house. He came through for me just after Thanksgiving, but after the hard time I had giving you a shawl, I waited for the right moment."

"It certainly was the right time," she whispered into his ear, then kissed him with a little smacking sound that made him shudder. "You made me realize that without you my dreams were empty illusions."

"You came here to be with me forever," he said, wanting to hear her say it.

"Yes, forever. I love you so much, Jason."

"I love you," he said solemnly, crushing her against him. "How do you feel about a small New Year's Day wedding in Aunt Rachel's parlor?"

"She'd adore it! We're one of her great successes as a matchmaker."

"No way! I made my own bid for you."

"Going, going, gone, darling," she whispered, not at all concerned that the map of Massachusetts would never be crisply folded again.

# LOOK FOR NEXT MONTH'S
# CANDLELIGHT ECSTASY ROMANCES®

A woman's place—the parlor, not the concert stage! But radiant Diana Ballantyne, pianist extraordinaire, had one year before she would bow to her father's wishes, return to England and marry. She had given her word, yet the moment she met the brilliant Maestro, Baron Lukas von Korda, her fate was sealed. He touched her soul with music, kissed her lips with fire, filled her with unnameable desire. One minute warm and passionate, the next aloof, he mystified her, tantalized her. She longed for artistic triumph, ached for surrender, her passions ignited by Vienna dreams.

A DELL BOOK    19530-6    $3.50

# Vienna Dreams

### by JANETTE RADCLIFFE